*A change of heart . . .*

Tim put the tips of his fingers together and swiveled slowly in his chair. "Nicole, we've never had an incident like this before. We're not entirely comfortable with our decision, but we feel we're going to have to let you go."

Nicole dug her fingernails into the arm of her chair to keep herself from crying. She couldn't believe her ears. They were letting her go. Firing her. After all those weeks when she had wanted to leave, she'd made it through. Now, it wasn't up to her. They didn't want *her* around.

A few weeks ago, leaving Camp Kissamee had seemed like a great idea. Until today, she'd never intended to stay. She'd hated it from day one. If they had fired her two weeks ago, she would have been only too happy to walk out, head held high.

But not now. Not now that she was beginning to feel as though she belonged. Deep down, she knew that she belonged here more than she did anywhere else—with people who actually seemed to care about her.

It didn't matter, though. It was too late. She was being fired.

# CAMP COUNSELORS

# CAMPFIRE SECRETS

## DIANE AMES

# HarperPaperbacks

*A Division of HarperCollinsPublishers*

HarperPaperbacks *A Division of* HarperCollins*Publishers*
10 East 53rd Street, New York, N.Y. 10022

Copyright © 1992 by Diane Ames
    and Daniel Weiss Associates, Inc.
Cover art copyright © 1992 by Daniel Weiss Associates, Inc.

Produced by Daniel Weiss Associates, Inc.
33 West 17th Street, New York, New York 10011.

First printing: July, 1992

Printed in the United States of America

HarperPaperbacks and colophon are trademarks of
HarperCollins*Publishers*

10 9 8 7 6 5 4 3 2 1

# CHAPTER
## ONE

"Hurry up, Nicole, or we'll be late for flagpole!" Lisa Siegel called from outside the bathroom on Thursday morning.

"Who cares," Nicole Talbot muttered in response as she brushed her raven-black hair. The idea of going to flagpole at seven thirty every morning wasn't exactly something that thrilled her. If she were at home in New York City, she would still be asleep, or at the very least, sipping orange juice and looking out over the city from her mother's penthouse apartment, where they'd lived ever since her parents' divorce. Instead, she was stuck in a cabin—with five other junior counselors, no less—that was so small it was nicknamed the Shack. The entire cabin was barely as big as her bedroom at home.

It wasn't as if she got along with everyone in the Shack, either. She and Jennifer Trowbridge couldn't stand each other. Jennifer's best friend, Annie Johnson, wasn't much better. Megan Pierce and Beth Rierdon weren't bad, but they were so into being counselors at Camp Kissamee, it was ridiculous. Lisa

1

was the only one Nicole could really talk to, but even she wasn't exactly Nicole's kind of person. Besides, ever since Lisa had started dating Michael Horst, another JC, he was all she could talk about.

Nicole definitely was not into spending her summer as a junior counselor at a camp hidden away in Vermont's Green Mountains. Sometimes she still had trouble believing she was there, even though it was the end of July, and camp was already half over. The first day she'd arrived in Middlebrook, Nicole had thought someone was playing an elaborate practical joke on her. The town consisted of one restaurant, one old movie theater, a bicycle shop, and a narrow runway that passed for a regional airport. Absolute Hicksville, as far as Nicole could see. She might as well be spending the summer under a rock.

She frowned, remembering the comedy of errors that had landed her, of all people, in a job as a junior counselor at a rustic Vermont summer camp. Nicole had had her seventeenth summer perfectly planned. With the help of some friends of her mother, she had snagged a summer internship at *Glamour* magazine. It was the perfect job for her. She loved fashion, and she had planned on doing some modeling herself one day. She'd been hoping that she could get to know the right people in the business and spend the summer hanging out at cool parties with them.

Then her mother had sprung the horrible news on her. She had been suffering from a back injury for the past few weeks, and suddenly she'd found a place in Arizona that was world famous for fixing bad backs. She announced to Nicole that she would be spending the entire summer in Arizona. Nicole didn't want her mother to be in pain, but she didn't see why she couldn't find a place in Manhattan that was just as good. Once her mother had told her her plans, Nicole had hoped she could live in Connecticut at her father's house—it would only be a short commute to the city from there. But her father was going to be spending a large part of the summer in Europe working at a company he'd just bought. That left Nicole without a place to stay for the summer. Of course, she'd suggested that they let her live in the Manhattan apartment by herself—but they didn't like that plan. That's when her father had come up with the idea for her to spend the summer at Camp Kissamee, where he'd gone over thirty years ago. He'd said it would be good for her, that it would help "build her character." Nicole didn't see how standing around in a meadow all afternoon teaching eight-year-old kids to shoot arrows in archery would build her character. But her mother had agreed—and before she knew what was happening, Nicole had gotten a job as a junior counselor and was on her way to Vermont.

It would be funny if it wasn't so horrible. Nicole couldn't remember her parents ever agreeing on *anything.* They hadn't seen eye to eye since they got divorced when she was twelve. This had to be the first time, and it was ruining *her* summer.

"Come on," Lisa said. "Brett's going to announce something big today. I don't want to miss it."

Nicole opened the bathroom door and stepped out. "Okay," she said with a sigh. "I'm ready." She grabbed a sweater from her bed and tied it around her shoulders. The mornings were cold at Camp Kissamee—too cold, in Nicole's opinion, for late July.

"I think we're going to start the Camp Kissamee Comps next week," Lisa said. "They were really fun last year."

"The whats?" Nicole asked as they made their way down the path toward the lawn in front of the Lodge where the flagpole was located.

"The Comps," Lisa said. "It's an all-camp competition, with two different teams. It's a tradition here. There's a whole bunch of different games—some of them are hilarious."

Nicole raised one eyebrow. "I'll bet," she muttered under her breath. Camp was bad enough without all these little traditions that they had to suffer through. Nicole had just experienced another Kissamee tradition, the annual Revue, which was a night of camper and counselor performances. Although it had turned out all right in the end, Nicole felt it was just one more illustration of the fact that she did not belong there. She'd recited a dramatic monologue, and what had everyone else done? There was a magic show, a couple of juvenile dancing performances, and some comedy routines. Lisa had finally gotten over her stage fright long enough to sing, and she'd been the only one with any real talent, besides herself.

Lisa and Nicole sat down in the small semicircle under the big oak tree where the JCs usually sat for flagpole. Brett Carver, head of the boys' camp, was just getting up to make his announcement. Mara Nye, head of the girls' camp, shot Nicole an irritated look as she sat down. Mara was a stickler for promptness, and everything else. She was always finding something wrong with the way Nicole did things.

"Don't look now, but Mara's giving us the evil eye," Lisa said.

"When doesn't she?" Nicole replied. She pulled her sweater over her head and looked around at all the campers. The girls in her cabin, Girls' Thirteen, were busy talking to one another, shielding their mouths with their hands. *Probably checking out some new boys,* Nicole thought. Almost all the thirteen-year-old girls in her cabin were completely boy crazy.

Nicole was a little boy crazy herself sometimes— at least back in the city, where there was something to look at. So far, the only guy she'd been interested in at camp had fallen for Annie instead. His name was Gil Osborne, he was from Australia, and he was gorgeous. Nicole still felt a pang whenever she saw Annie and Gil together, which was way too often. Since Gil, Nicole hadn't found anyone she was even remotely interested in. Brett wasn't bad-looking, but he was too all-American, Nicole thought as she watched him adjust his trademark baseball cap. Anyway, he, too, had recently started dating another counselor.

"All right! I have some good news, and some bad news," Brett began. "The good news is that Kissamee Comps start this Monday! The whole camp will be divided up into two teams. Each team will be made up of campers and counselors, and cabins will be separated. There are about twenty different events, so if your team falls behind, you'll have a chance to catch up. We'll have several days' worth of contests—relays, soccer, volleyball, water sports, and general all-out fighting to be the Supreme Team. Wednesday night we'll announce the winner and wrap up Camp Comps with an all-camp party. Now, all this will be happening in addition to our regular activities, so it's going to be pretty busy around here next week!"

"What's the bad news?" yelled one camper.

"I was getting to that," Brett said. "On Sunday night, after we hand out the lists of teams—chosen completely at random, of course—Wally's promised to make us a big cookout here on the lawn."

Several people laughed, while others groaned. Nicole felt her stomach turn over. Wally was the camp cook, and he'd been working at Camp Kissamee for about twenty years. With all that experience, Nicole thought he *should* be good at cooking, but half the time his food was inedible. He seemed to think that just because little kids liked hot dogs, it was okay to serve them several times a week. Once Nicole had asked him to make her a chef's salad instead, and he'd laughed.

"If I eat another hot dog this summer, I'm going to die," Jennifer said.

"No kidding," Megan said.

"But we're trying to convince him to make barbecued chicken this time," Brett continued. "So remember—on Sunday, there'll be a cookout here instead of dinner, and we'll hand out sheets with the teams on them. Get psyched for the great Camp Kissamee Comps!"

*Psyched?* Nicole thought. Just the thought of the stupid competition made her yawn. She couldn't understand how anyone could get so excited about it. She only half listened to everyone around her talking excitedly about the Comps.

"Nicole, have you ever done anything like this?" Lisa asked with a bright smile.

"No, thank God," Nicole said.

"Oh, I forgot—the queen doesn't like sports," Jennifer teased her. "You might get your silk shorts dirty, Nicole. You'd better go down to the army/navy store and get some green fatigues fast."

"Yeah, right. I'm really going to take fashion tips from you, Jennifer," Nicole shot back. Jennifer wore the same exact thing every day: khaki hiking shorts, a baggy T-shirt, and beat-up high-top sneakers. She was extremely athletic and worked down on the waterfront teaching swimming and patrolling as a lifeguard. The only thing that saved her from being a total drag, as far as Nicole could see, was her sense of humor. Even though Jennifer's digs were usually directed her way, Nicole had to admit that some of them were good.

"Let's go eat breakfast," Annie said. "Arguing on an empty stomach is no fun." She started walking toward the Lodge, gesturing to Jennifer to follow her. That was typical of Annie, Nicole thought. She never wanted to see anyone argue—she was always trying to make everyone in the Shack get along. Well, Nicole wasn't going to be nice to everybody. She might not win the Best Junior Counselor award, and Tim and Cathy Maddox, the camp directors, might not ask her to come back next summer, but she didn't care. This was the first and *last* summer she planned to spend at Camp Kissamee.

Megan, Beth, and Lisa went off to join their cabins, and Nicole waited for hers to catch up with her on the Lodge steps. As everyone filed past her into the dining room, she looked out at the mountains above her. Pale sunlight filtered through the pine trees. It was almost pretty.

"What, aren't you eating today?"

Nicole looked at Eliot Packard, who was standing in front of her, smiling.

"If you don't hurry, you'll miss Wally's famous buckwheat pancakes," Eliot said. "Trust me—the guys in my cabin could eat them all."

Nicole smiled faintly. Eliot was one of the few

8

other junior counselors, besides Lisa, that she felt she could talk to. He came from New York City, too, where his father was a Broadway producer. Tall, blue-eyed, with light brown hair cut stylishly so that it was long on top and short in the back, Eliot wasn't bad-looking. He just wasn't that exciting. From what Nicole could see, he went in for all this camp stuff as much as everyone else.

"I think I'll survive without Wally's pancakes," Nicole answered. "Though I'm not sure I really want to survive, at this point."

Eliot looked confused. "Are you trying to say you're not dying to win the three-legged race next week?"

Nicole stared at him. "Three-legged race? Are you kidding?"

Eliot shook his head. "Afraid not."

"I can't believe this place!" Nicole said. "They want us to act like children, too."

"Well, it *is* a camp," Eliot said. "I'd better get in there before my kids trash the dining room. Hey, my dad's coming up this weekend. How about your folks?"

"No, they can't make it," Nicole said. "Tell your dad to bring some bagels. I would absolutely *kill* for a good bagel."

Eliot laughed. "Me, too. He said he's bringing a lot of stuff, but knowing him it'll probably just be reading material—like a bunch of scripts he's considering producing. Well, see you." He went inside just as Zoe Brown, one of the girls in Nicole's cabin, ran up the steps.

"Hey, Nicole. What team do you want to be on?" Zoe asked. "We heard we're going to have to wear different colors. I want to be purple, because it looks best on me."

"Yeah, but blue looks better on me," Janet Cunningham added.

"You're not going to wear the color all the time," said Dee Gordon, the head counselor of Girls' Thirteen. "Unless of course you want me to paint it on you!" Dee worked in arts and crafts with Annie. She was nice, if a little too enthusiastic for Nicole's taste.

"What color do you want to be, Nicole?" asked Marian Drew.

*None,* Nicole thought. "It really doesn't matter to me," she said, trying to sound like a counselor, since Dee was listening.

"I hope we're on the same team," said Mimi Krantz, pulling out a chair next to Nicole at their table in the dining room. Compared with the rest of the girls in the cabin, Mimi was incredibly quiet, and a little on the shy side. When the other campers got involved in some scheme—a raid on another cabin, or a practical joke on someone—Mimi usually stayed out of it.

Nicole smiled at her as she put a pancake on her plate. "Me, too," she said. Mimi was sweet, and she was not nearly as difficult to handle as the rest of the girls.

10

Nicole felt a tap on her shoulder. "Nicole, could I have a word with you?" Mara asked.

*Oh, great,* Nicole thought. *Here comes another lecture.* She pushed back her chair and stood up, then followed Mara to a corner of the dining room, away from the tables. "What is it?" she asked, trying to sound as polite as she could.

"You were late to flagpole this morning," Mara said. She brushed a miniature piece of lint off her neat khaki shorts, which looked as if they had just been ironed.

"I was?" Nicole asked. "I thought I got there right at seven thirty. That's what Lisa's watch said, anyway."

Mara frowned. "Well, you were five minutes late. This is the third or fourth time I've had to talk to you about this, Nicole. *Everyone* needs to be there at seven thirty, and that includes you."

"I'll tell Lisa her watch is wrong," Nicole said with a shrug. "Sorry."

"I hope this is the last time I have to remind you that promptness is required at all camp activities," Mara said. "As a junior counselor, you should be setting an example for the campers. Please try to be on time in the future."

"Right." Nicole returned to her table and sank into her chair. She took a bite of her pancake, which was already cold.

"What was that all about?" asked Dee.

"I was a couple of minutes late to flagpole,"

Nicole answered. "Mara practically wants to put me in jail for it." *As if I'm not in jail already*, Nicole thought. She was getting pretty tired of all the rules and regulations at camp, and the way Mara checked up on her all the time, like she was a little kid.

"Oh, you know how she is." Dee laughed. "I think she should become an army sergeant when camp is over. So what are you doing for Dead Day on Saturday?"

Dead Day was the one day during the summer that all the JCs had completely off at the same time. Once a week they had a free day from after breakfast until dinner, but this was the only time when they'd all be off for most of the day and able to do things together. Nicole hadn't made any plans, though. She didn't want to hang out with anyone, especially. She could take the bus to Boston, but it would take so long that by the time she got there, she'd have to head back. A lot of parents were visiting, but not hers, of course.

"I don't know," Nicole said. "I might go to the Abbey and watch a movie if anything decent's playing. I want to lie out in the sun and maybe make some phone calls."

"Sounds good," Dee said.

"I wish I could *go* somewhere," Nicole said.

"Let's go shopping—you can take us along, too, can't you?" Marian pleaded.

"Guys, the whole point of Dead Day is for Nicole to have time to herself," Dee reminded them.

12

"Besides, I don't have a car, remember?" Nicole said. She had never felt so stuck before in all her life. Ever since she'd gotten to camp, she'd been trying to think of a way she could get out of it. She could pretend to be sick, but her parents would insist that she see the best doctors right away and discover she was perfectly fine. She could break a leg or something, but that would hurt too much. What if she convinced her father to fly her to Europe to meet him? The morning she got there, they'd have breakfast at some tiny sidewalk cafe in Paris, then head for the Louvre and look at the paintings.

Nicole took a sip of watery orange juice and glanced over at a table of ten-year-old boys who were shouting and flinging food at one another. The only painting in sight was an eight-year-old's watercolor of the camp lake.

Camp Kissamee was a far cry from the Louvre, and from everything else that civilization had to offer, as far as Nicole was concerned. She couldn't wait until the end of August, when it would be all over and she'd get her life back.

*If I last that long,* Nicole thought as the girls in her cabin started arguing about which one of them was better at horseback riding. It wasn't going to be easy.

# CHAPTER
## TWO

"No way. He didn't."

"He says he did." Jennifer tossed a knapsack onto her bed and started stuffing clothes into it. She and Annie were alone in the Shack during rest hour, which they had free every afternoon after lunch, while the campers napped, read books, or wrote letters.

"How could he even *think* about asking Nicole out again?" Annie shook her head. "Is Andy a glutton for punishment or something?"

Jennifer shrugged. "I guess he's really hooked on her." Jennifer's good friend Andy Brenner had had a wicked crush on Nicole ever since camp started. Jennifer had tried to warn him about her, let him know that Nicole was simply using him to get Gil's attention, but he hadn't believed her until it was too late. When he finally realized the truth, though, Jennifer had hoped Andy was through with Nicole for good. "I guess I'll never understand boys," she said to Annie.

"Maybe it's just a case of temporary insanity," Annie said. "I bet he'll change his mind tomorrow when he remembers the way she treated him. Or maybe he was just teasing you."

"I *hope* so," Jennifer said. "I don't know how much more of Andy's lovesickness I can take." She rolled up a pair of wool socks and stuck them in the knapsack.

"I bet it'll feel good to get away," Annie said. "Where are you going on your overnight? I forgot."

"Granite Lake."

"Who else is going?"

"Brett's cabin," Jennifer said. "Just think—two weeks ago I would have been in heaven!" She laughed. She had decided she had a crush on Brett, and she'd written him a bunch of letters with the help of the head counselor in her cabin, Darcy Matthews. Actually, Darcy had written the letters—Jennifer couldn't think of anything to say, and she was too shy to approach Brett directly. She shouldn't have been too surprised when Brett ended up falling for Darcy instead of her! As it turned out, Darcy liked him, too, and the two of them were now dating.

So far, Jennifer's plan to find a boyfriend that summer had been a total failure. Before she'd even come to camp, she'd decided that this would be her summer to fall in love. She was sick of being the only one of her friends who didn't have a boyfriend. First she'd been interested in Charlie Fisher, a JC whom she nicknamed "Mr. Hollywood" because of his trademark sunglasses and linen blazer. Even though she'd been crazy about Charlie, he'd barely even noticed her—or the fact that she liked him. Then she'd come up with her disastrous Brett plan. After that, Jennifer had decided to take a break from her boyfriend hunt. Obviously, this wasn't going to be her summer for love.

"Anyone else going on the overnight?" asked Annie.

"Mara said she might assign another cabin or two —she was waiting to find out if there were enough vans to take us. Plus, we need to bring canoes." Jennifer screwed the cap of her toothpaste on extra tightly, then tossed it into the knapsack.

The back door of the Shack swung open, and they heard the old bed springs creaking as someone sat down. "A *fishing* trip?" Nicole said angrily. "Give me a break!"

Jennifer felt her back stiffen. She couldn't believe it. From the sound of things, Nicole would be accompanying her on the overnight to Granite Lake. "So much for getting away from things," Jennifer whispered.

"Boys' Thirteen and Girls' Thirteen—that ought to be fun," Annie said, rolling her eyes.

The bed springs creaked again, and a moment later Nicole stood in the doorway that separated the back room she and Lisa shared from the rest of the cabin. "I didn't know anyone was here," she said, pushing her silky black hair back from her face.

16

"Did I hear you say something about a fishing trip?" Jennifer asked.

"Yes." Nicole groaned. "Mara just told me our cabin's going, and we have to be ready in an hour. I like sushi, but I don't want to *catch* any."

"Don't worry, you probably won't," Jennifer said.

Nicole frowned at her. "I don't see why anyone enjoys it, anyway."

"Come on, the part where you cut the fish open and take out the eyes is really fun," Jennifer said.

"You probably do like to do that," Nicole replied. "Anyway, what am I supposed to bring?"

"Sweater, sleeping bag—you know, all the outdoor stuff you have," Annie said.

"Yeah, and don't forget your blow dryer," Jennifer said. "You might find a tree you could plug it into."

"Very funny," Nicole said. "I can tell this is going to be a blast." She walked back into the back bedroom.

"Tell me about it," Jennifer muttered, with a pleading look at Annie. "Are you sure you don't want to go in my place? I'll pay you."

"It won't be that bad," Annie said. "It's only one night. When you get back, the next day will be Dead Day and your parents will be here to take us out to lunch, remember?"

"Only one night, she says." Jennifer shook her head. "I guess I'll just have to make the best of it, as my mother would say."

"Just promise me one thing," Annie said softly. "Make sure you and Nicole share a tent, okay?"

Jennifer punched her playfully on the arm, and Annie laughed. "Sure, it's funny to you!" With any luck, there would be so much to do that Jennifer wouldn't even notice Nicole was around. If three or four cabins were going, there'd be plenty of people in between her and Nicole.

"Jen, do you think you could fit this in your bag?" Nicole stood in the doorway, holding the pillow from her bed. "I can't sleep on the ground unless I have a pillow."

"No way!" Jennifer said. "What do I look like, anyway—your personal valet? This isn't the Plaza Hotel."

"Obviously." Nicole went back into her room and threw the pillow onto her bed.

Jennifer took a deep breath and prepared herself for what was going to be a long, aggravating night.

Fishing. Nicole couldn't wait to tell her friends in New York about this. She'd been dropped off with ten thirteen-year-old girls and three canoes in the middle of nowhere. Fortunately Dee was along, too, to build the fire and set up the tents. Along with her cabin, Jennifer was there with Darcy and Girls' Nine, and Brett had come with his cabin and Josh Phillips, the JC for Boys' Thirteen. They were setting up camp next to Granite Lake, where they'd spend that afternoon and the next morning fishing.

Nicole didn't plan to get near any fish hooks. The only thing she wanted to do was take a swim and relax. She had to admit, though, that it felt good to be off camp grounds, even if she was only thirty miles away. She stretched her arms over her head and took a deep breath of the fragrant mountain air.

"Nicole, could you help me with the fishing poles?" Dee asked. She was struggling to get them out of the back of the van.

Nicole walked over and pulled out a bunch of poles that were tied together. She wrinkled her nose. "They stink already."

"What did you expect—new poles?" Brett said with a laugh. He walked past, carrying a load of firewood.

Nicole didn't bother to answer him. She had decided that she wasn't going to let anyone get on her nerves—otherwise, she knew she would never survive the overnight.

"Who wants to go for a swim?" Jennifer called from the shore of the lake. She was standing on a rock, wearing her racing swimsuit, with her long, brown hair tied back in a ponytail.

"Me!" Several of the campers answered, scrambling out of tents with their bathing suits already on. Nicole lugged the poles down to the lakeside.

"Nicole, you'd better change—we all need to lifeguard," Jennifer told her.

Nicole glanced up at Jennifer. "Excuse me, but I didn't know that you were in charge."

Jennifer shrugged. "I'm just doing my job. If you want Dee or Brett to tell you, then go ahead and wait. The fact is that there are over thirty kids here who want to swim, and we have to watch all of them."

Nicole was about to say something when Mimi came up and stood beside her. "Nicole, will you help me swim?" she said.

Mimi was learning to swim that summer. She was taking beginning swimming and making slow progress, from what Nicole had seen. "Sure," Nicole said. "Let me change into my suit. I'll be right back." All the counselors at camp were required to be certified in lifesaving. So far Nicole had only had to lifeguard a few times. She wished she were teaching swimming instead of archery—at least then she'd be near the water all day instead of stuck in a hot meadow with prickly, dry grass underfoot and bees buzzing around her face.

She went up to her tent, crouched down, and crawled inside. It was nearly impossible to get dressed in a tent that was only three feet high, but somehow Nicole managed. *If my friends at home could see me now!* she thought. She could hear shrieks down at the lake's edge—the boys were probably splashing the girls, as usual. She reached inside her bag to pull out some sunscreen. She couldn't find it at first, so she rummaged around in the outside pocket until—

"*Aaaaaaaah!*" Nicole screamed and ran out of the

20

tent. There was something wet and slimy in her bag, and she did *not* want to know what it was.

Dee ran over to her. "What is it? What's wrong?"

"There's something in my—my bag," she said, wiping her hand off on the grass.

"Like what?" asked Dee.

"Like—a dead fish," Nicole said.

"You're kidding!" Dee went into the tent and came out carrying the bag. "Where is it?"

Nicole pointed to the outside pocket.

Dee peeked inside, then put her hand in, pulling out a long, thick worm. "Yuck! Well, at least it'll make good bait." She dropped it into one of the jars full of worms that they had unloaded.

*Wait a second,* Nicole thought. *We didn't bring any jars of worms—they were in the other van. The one Jennifer was in.* She marched down to the water's edge. "Don't think you'll get away with a dumb prank like that," she told Jennifer.

Jennifer cupped her hands over her mouth. "Hey, Donny, cut it out!" she yelled to a boy from Brett's cabin who was relentlessly splashing one of the nine-year-old girls. Then she turned to Nicole, an innocent expression on her face. "What are you talking about? What prank?"

"You know what I'm talking about," Nicole said. "There was a worm in my bag, and you put it there." Her resolve not to let anything bother her had vanished in the last two minutes. If Jennifer thought Nicole would put up with her juvenile pranks, she

21

was wrong. "I don't think Mara will think it was very funny, either," she said.

"Nicole, I really don't know what you're making such a big deal about. So a worm crawled into your bag—we are outdoors, you know," Jennifer said.

Nicole walked away and stood on another rock to get a clearer view of the campers in the water. Mimi was keeping close to shore, with both hands on the sandy bottom, kicking her legs through the water. Zoe, Marian, and Janet were all farther out, treading water in a circle and talking. The other girls in her cabin were swimming around or sitting on rocks sunbathing.

If Nicole weren't so angry at Jennifer, she might even be enjoying herself, relaxing in the sun far away from the tedium of the camp day. She couldn't believe what Jennifer had done. It was so completely immature to go around pulling dumb pranks like that—and she did it constantly, too, like the time Nicole's bed had been short-sheeted a few weeks ago. She knew Jennifer had been responsible, but then she wouldn't even admit she had done it! Nicole didn't know how much longer she could take living with someone who despised her so much that she wanted to make her miserable. Of course, she hadn't been serious about going to Mara about the worm. Nicole was not a tattletale. She could deal with this herself. But how?

Nicole stared over at Jennifer, who was talking to Josh Phillips and laughing. In a way, she and Jennifer weren't that different. Jennifer was pretty, too, and she would look even prettier if she ever wore anything besides baggy clothes. She was self-confident, like Nicole. Sometimes Nicole thought that, of everyone in the Shack, Jennifer was the most likely candidate to become her friend. But that was impossible—Jennifer and Annie were already best friends, and they obviously weren't interested in including her.

*I wish I could get out of here,* Nicole thought, gazing out at the water. She'd been fantasizing about leaving ever since she'd arrived at camp—ever since the day she'd walked into the Shack and burst into tears. No one seemed to understand that being at camp felt like being in prison to her. She didn't know if she could take another four weeks that were as lousy as the first four.

*Maybe I'll call Mother tomorrow and see what she says.* Nicole was sure that once she explained how unhappy and lonely she was, her mother would be bound to feel sorry for her. Maybe she would come to visit. Maybe she would even pick her up and take her back to Manhattan.

"Okay, who's ready to catch some fish?" Brett yelled.

As the boys struggled to be first out of the water, Nicole scratched a mosquito bite on her foot. Yes, it was definitely time to start thinking about getting out of Vermont—the sooner, the better!

# CHAPTER
## THREE

"It was bad enough that someone put a worm in my bag. Now I have *marsh*mallow in my hair." Nicole was sitting in her tent trying to get a comb through her hair. After dinner, they had all sat around the campfire roasting marshmallows.

"It's not that bad. You just look as if you ran into a jar of Fluff, that's all." Zoe giggled.

Nicole glared at her. "Thanks a lot. I could *kill* that kid, whatever his name is." One of the thirteen-year-old boys had been chasing Casey Koller, a girl in her cabin, trying to put a marshmallow in her hair. It had landed in Nicole's instead.

"Donny," Janet added. "Donny McRae."

"Maybe you should try some Vaseline," Marian suggested.

"Put grease in my hair? No thanks." Nicole shook her head.

"Then how are you going to get it out?" asked Marian. "It's still stuck, isn't it?"

Nicole tugged at a clump of marshmallow. It

squished through her fingers and spread to even more of her hair.

"We could cut off that part of your hair," Zoe said. "I had to do that once when I got bubble gum in my hair."

"No, thanks. I don't feel like having a haircut right now," Nicole snapped. "Give me the Vaseline." Marian handed her a small jar, and Nicole took out a gob of it and started to work it into her hair.

"That looks good," Janet said.

Nicole ignored her. She kept working the Vaseline through the sticky clump of hair. Gradually, she pulled off strings of marshmallow. To her dismay, they were covered with hair. "Great, I'll probably be bald on that side of my head now," she grumbled.

"Want to wear my hat?" Marian held out a baseball cap with the logo from a popular TV show on the front of it.

"No, thanks." Nicole finally pulled the last bit of marshmallow out of her hair. "I'm going to wash my hair."

"You can't," Zoe said. "There's no shower here."

"No, but there is a lake," Nicole replied, looking for her towel in her overnight bag.

"You can't wash your hair in the lake!" Janet said. "Not with regular shampoo, anyway. You need that special stuff that doesn't make any suds."

Nicole sighed. Janet was right. Besides, it was too cold to go for a swim—and too dark. Great, now she actually had to be seen with gobs of grease in her hair. She should have just left the marshmallow in. She turned off her flashlight, slid farther down in her sleeping bag, and pulled it up around her neck. She'd had just about enough of the overnight—no, more than enough. She never thought she'd be dying to get back to camp, but she definitely was ready.

Janet, Marian, and Zoe were whispering loudly in one corner of the tent, all crowded onto one sleeping bag. "Keep it down. I'm trying to sleep," Nicole told them. *It figures,* Nicole thought. *I'm stuck in a tiny tent with the three loudest girls at camp.*

Nicole reached down to scratch her newest mosquito bite. Then her other foot started itching. Then her legs. Nicole couldn't imagine how she could have gotten so many mosquito bites in one day. She'd been wearing extra-strong insect repellent.

"Nicole, what are you *do*ing?" Zoe called.

"I think I was attacked by a horde of mosquitoes!" Nicole answered. She was furiously scratching her knee.

"Do you itch all over?" asked Marian.

"All over my legs," Nicole replied. "It's driving me crazy!"

"Uh oh." Janet scooted over to the sleeping bag next to Nicole's. "It might not be mosquito bites."

Nicole looked over at her. "Then what—"

"Oh no! Poison ivy!" Zoe screeched.

Nicole practically leaped out of her sleeping bag.

"Everything all right in there?" Jennifer called through the small vent at the end of the tent.

26

"No, it's not," Nicole said. "I think I have poison ivy."

"Really? Let me take a look at it." Jennifer unzipped the tent opening and crawled in. "Where?"

"Here." Nicole pointed to her legs. "And on my feet, too."

"I don't see any bumps," Jennifer said. "What's this?" She brushed at some powder on Nicole's ankle. "Is that baby powder?"

"No, I didn't put any on," Nicole said.

Jennifer rubbed the powder on her hand. A few seconds later, she began to scratch her hand. "It's itching powder!" she said. "Congratulations, Nicole. You've now been on an official Camp Kissamee overnight. Everyone gets the itching-powder treatment sooner or later."

Nicole glowered at her. "Oh, thanks a lot. I'm so honored."

"Hey, *I* didn't have anything to do with this." Jennifer scratched the back of her hand. "Do you think I would have put any on me if I did? This is going to drive me crazy. I'm going to wash it off, and I suggest you do the same thing." She opened the tent and stepped out. Nicole heard her walk toward the lake, crunching branches underfoot.

If Jennifer hadn't done it, then . . . Nicole turned to Janet, Marian, and Zoe, who were gathered in one corner of the tent. "Okay, guys. Very funny."

"What are you talking about?" Zoe replied, looking calm.

"I know you did it, so why don't you just apologize now, before I tell Dee what happened." Nicole rubbed her feet together.

Marian giggled. "We didn't do anything."

"Are you sure Jennifer didn't do it?" Janet asked. "If you ask me, she looked incredibly guilty."

Nicole stared at each girl, trying to read their expressions. Were they telling the truth? She didn't know them well enough to decide. "Okay, fine. You didn't do it. But when I find out who did, she's in big trouble." She crawled out of the tent and started to walk down to the lake. She could hear giggling coming from her tent as she left, and as she passed some of the other tents she heard laughter, too.

*I'm glad everyone else is having so much fun,* she thought, bending over to splash some water on her grease-coated hair. Then she walked around in the lake for a minute, hoping the water would dissolve the itching powder on her legs and feet. *Some overnight,* she thought. *Itching powder, marshmallow in her hair, worms in her bag . . .* Could it get any worse?

Jennifer held a stick with a marshmallow on the end of it above the fire. All the campers had finally gone to bed, and she wanted to have a few minutes alone before she went into her tent. She smiled, thinking of the look on Nicole's face when she found out she'd been "powdered." Her campers had done the same thing to her last year when she was a counselor-in-training.

"Mind if I join you?"

Jennifer smiled at Josh, who was standing on the other side of the small fire. "No, go ahead."

He took a marshmallow out of the bag, then slid it onto a stick and started to roast it over the fire. "I didn't get a chance to have one before, it was such a madhouse out here."

Jennifer nodded. "I'm glad everyone's having a good time, though."

"Except Nicole." Josh laughed. "She wouldn't even eat any of the trout we caught. I think she had potato chips for dinner."

"She was still recovering from her close encounter with a jumbo worm," Jennifer said, smiling. She took the stick out of the fire and sampled the browned marshmallow.

Josh watched her. "How do you know it was a jumbo worm? All she said was that it was a worm."

"I have my sources," Jennifer said. She popped the rest of the marshmallow in her mouth.

"As in, you know how big it was because you put it there, right?" Josh grinned.

"Well . . . maybe," Jennifer said.

Josh laughed. "I can't believe you! I mean, Nicole gets on everyone's nerves sometimes, but no one ever has the guts to get her back for it."

"You should see what her cabin did tonight,"

Jennifer said. "They put itching powder in her sleeping bag."

"Is that why she was just in the lake?" Josh asked.

Jennifer nodded. "I don't blame those girls, though. After the way Nicole's been acting all summer, she deserves a few practical jokes. I'm tired of her complaining all the time and telling other people what to do. Maybe it'll make her lighten up a little. She acts like such a princess."

Jennifer knew she sounded harsh, but that was how she felt. A month of putting up with Nicole was enough already. What made it even worse was that sometimes Nicole acted as if she *might* be human. That made Jennifer think she wasn't such a bad person, after all. Then she'd turn around and do something like ask Jennifer to carry her pillow, or demand that she get the best tent site. Nicole thought she was better than everyone else, and Jennifer was sick of it! She'd thought Nicole might mellow out a little bit as the summer went on, but she was acting just as cold as she had the first day she arrived.

"Jennifer, you know how we're going to have a hayride because the last one was canceled?" Josh asked.

Jennifer nodded. The JCs were supposed to have had a hayride a few weeks ago, but it had been called off when Charlie Fisher and Beth Rierdon got into a car accident on their way to meet everybody. Charlie and Beth were both okay, although Charlie's arm was still in a sling. "It's the weekend after this one," Jennifer said. "Sunday night, I think."

"Yeah. Well, I was just wondering if, uh, you're going," Josh said.

"Sure I'm going," Jennifer said. She gazed into the fire. It would be nice if she had someone to go with—it would be so romantic. Annie had Gil, and now Lisa was dating Michael . . . they were so lucky. "Josh! Your marshmallow!" she cried.

Flames had engulfed the stick, which Josh quickly dropped into the fire. "Whoops. I guess I wasn't paying attention," he said.

"Here." Jennifer stood up and handed him her stick. "I'm going to turn in. See you tomorrow, okay?"

Josh looked up at her. He seemed a little flustered, but Jennifer couldn't imagine why. "Yeah. Good night," he mumbled.

A minute later, while Jennifer was snuggling into her sleeping bag, she heard Josh dump sand on the fire to put it out. Next to her, one of her campers was snoring softly. Jennifer wished she were sharing her tent with Annie, so they could stay up talking. She felt as though she'd hardly spent any time with her best friend, even though they shared the same bunk bed. Lately, Annie was doing everything with Gil instead of with her. Jennifer could understand why, but it still hurt sometimes. Well, maybe next year she'd have a boyfriend of her own.

\* \* \*

"The great fisherwoman returns!" Michael Horst, Lisa's boyfriend, called out as Nicole walked into the Barn on Friday afternoon.

She looked at him and raised one eyebrow. "Hardly." They had returned from the overnight just before lunch, which Nicole had skipped so that she could take a shower and wash off all the junk she'd accumulated on her skin and hair. She hadn't really wanted to hang out at the Barn with everyone—the second floor was the official "Counselors' Lounge" and unofficial hangout spot for the JCs after lunch every day. But she couldn't think of anything else to do, either, and she didn't want to hang around the Shack.

"How was the trip?" Lisa asked.

"I don't want to talk about it." Nicole sank into one of the old overstuffed chairs.

"That good, huh?" Eliot grinned at her.

"I had a great time," Jennifer said, opening a can of soda. "Granite Lake is so beautiful."

"How many?" Andy Brenner asked with an exaggerated sigh.

"What do you mean?" Gil leaned forward on the couch, which he was sharing with Annie. Nicole still felt a tingle when she heard Gil's voice—she loved his Australian accent. She had to keep reminding herself to stay away from him. He was clearly going to be with Annie for the rest of the summer.

"What I mean is, if she had a good time, then she must have caught a lot of fish," Andy said. "And she's not going to miss an opportunity to brag about it."

Jennifer looked shocked. "Me? Brag?"

Annie laughed. "Yes, you. Come on, Jen. Go ahead."

"She caught five," Josh said, smiling. "And that was two more than anyone else."

"And one more than I caught last year," Jennifer said. "Just for the record."

Nicole sighed. "I'm sure *The Guinness Book of World Records* is dying to hear from you. Why don't you run over to the Lodge and call them right now before someone else breaks the record?" Eliot started to laugh, and Nicole smiled at him in triumph.

"Of course, Nicole was too busy painting her nails to actually catch a fish," Jennifer replied.

Josh laughed. "And cleaning marshmallow out of her hair."

Nicole glared at him. Was Josh on Jennifer's side now, too? Did everyone at camp have to hate her?

"What happened?" asked Annie.

"It's a long story, but let's just say it'll be a long time before I spend an evening with a bunch of thirteen-year-old boys again," Nicole complained. "Talk about immature."

"What do you expect?" Eliot asked. "They *are* only thirteen."

Nicole frowned at him. Not even *Eliot* sympathized with her. She'd had the worst night of her life,

33

and nobody cared. They all thought it was a big joke. She would bet that if anything had happened to Annie, or Jennifer, or even Lisa, everyone would be acting all concerned. But because she was the one, they thought it was funny.

"When I was thirteen, I never acted like that," Michael said, looking around the room with a snooty expression on his face.

Lisa hit him playfully on the leg. "Yeah, you were probably worse."

"Horst, I have news for you. You're *still* worse," Eliot said.

"Hey, no fair. I'm a very mature junior counselor now!"

"What's everyone doing for Dead Day?" Lisa asked, shaking her head at Michael.

"Annie and I are going out to lunch with my parents," Jennifer announced—a little too smugly, in Nicole's opinion. Jennifer knew Nicole's parents weren't coming. "Then we're going to an amusement park, I think."

"Josh and I are going to eat as much as we can at my parents' house," Andy said. "And watch some baseball on TV."

Nicole couldn't believe it. If her parents came to visit, she'd certainly make more of the day than everyone else apparently was planning to. But at least their parents were showing up. That was more than she could say for hers.

"What about you, Nicole? Going to shop till you drop?" Lisa smiled.

"I doubt it. The only thing to buy in this town is cow feed," Nicole said.

"And milk," Michael said. "Don't forget milk."

"Please, if I drink any more milk I'm going to—"

"Turn into a cow?" Jennifer interrupted. Everyone started laughing.

Nicole sighed and got up from her chair. She was glad that everyone else found Jennifer's little comments so amusing. But she'd had about as many of them as she could take for one rest hour. Without saying good-bye, she walked out of the lounge and down the stairs.

Just outside the Barn, she ran into Mara. "Nicole, are you feeling all right?" Mara asked.

*Not if you consider the fact that I'm miserable at this place,* Nicole thought. "Sure. Why?"

"Well, I didn't see you at lunch," Mara said. "Where were you?"

"Oh, I had to take a shower," Nicole answered. "I had this grease in my hair and—"

"But you know that your presence is required at all meals," Mara said, "whether you sit with your cabin or not. That's a rule here. Nicole, have you ever read your rule book?"

"Of course!" Nicole said. She'd skimmed it at least once, anyway. "Look, Mara, you don't understand. I was on this overnight, right? And—"

"I'm afraid you're the one who doesn't

understand. Nicole, those rules exist for a reason. We need the JCs at lunch to watch the campers."

"Oh." Nicole nodded. "I guess I didn't think it through."

Mara consulted the clipboard that seemed as if it were permanently attached to her arm. "To make up for missing lunch, I have a chore for you to do. Wally needs someone to mop the kitchen floor this afternoon." She glanced at her watch. "If you hurry, you can get it done by one thirty."

"What?" Nicole decided she must have fallen asleep during rest hour and was in the middle of a bad dream.

"I'll escort you over there," Mara said, starting to walk toward the Lodge.

Nicole just stood there, not moving. Her? Mop?

"Nicole? It's a big kitchen, and you don't have much time," Mara said. "You'd better hurry."

How did anyone expect her to live through such an awful summer? Nicole wondered as she trudged after Mara. What next? Would she be expected to mow the entire lawn or clean all the horse stables? How could they *make* her eat lunch, anyway?

Exasperated, Nicole ran her hands through her hair. The part where the marshmallow had been still felt greasy. It had been impossible to get all the Vaseline out. But what difference did it make? She was only going to get filthy mopping up the kitchen floor. *I feel like Cinderella!* she thought, following Mara into the kitchen.

"Here's your helper," Mara said, smiling at Wally.

"Great!" The camp cook held out a huge metal pail with a wooden handle. "Fill this up, and I'll get the mop for you."

Nicole sighed and took the bucket from him. "Gee, thanks." She couldn't wait to call and tell her mother how miserable she was. Once her mother heard she had been forced to mop the kitchen floor, Nicole was sure she'd be on the first plane to Vermont. And then, with any luck, Nicole would be on the first plane *out*.

# CHAPTER
## FOUR

Saturday morning, Nicole was the first one to wake up in the Shack. It was Dead Day, and she didn't intend to waste her day off. Besides, she had to get off camp grounds before Mara asked her to do another obnoxious chore.

Nicole loved Saturdays, or at least she did back home. She usually slept late and then met some friends at Saks or downtown in Soho to do some shopping. Half the time they didn't buy anything, but that didn't matter. Nicole loved to hang around, to see and be seen. She didn't think hanging out at Ryan's, the only restaurant in downtown Middlebrook, would be quite the same, but she had decided to give it a try. She'd thought about hiring a taxi to take her to the closest mall, but it was too far away—she didn't want to spend all her money getting there. On top of everything else, her parents had put her on a measly allowance for the summer. So, she'd be spending the day in Middlebrook. But at least she'd have some time to herself, and she'd be getting away from camp.

"Nicole, what are you doing up so early?" Lisa yawned and stretched her arms over her head. She was still lying in bed. "It's Dead Day. We don't even have to go to flagpole."

"I'm going into town to have breakfast at Ryan's," Nicole said.

"Really? How are you getting there?" Lisa asked.

"Mara told me there are some bikes down in the Barn that I could use. I really miss going out to breakfast—my mother and I have brunch together almost every Sunday," Nicole said. After breakfast, she was going to call her mother from Ryan's, where she'd have the privacy to tell her she wanted to leave.

"That sounds nice." Lisa rolled over. "My parents are coming at around ten. Are you sure you don't want to come to lunch with us?"

Lisa had asked Nicole earlier in the week if she wanted to go along with her, her parents, and Michael to an expensive lunch at a restaurant in a neighboring town. Somehow, it didn't sound like a whole lot of fun to Nicole, but she appreciated being asked. "No, thanks, Lisa. I think I'd rather hang out by myself today."

"Okay," Lisa said, "but if you change your mind, meet us here at about noon."

Nicole quickly got dressed. Since she was going to ride a bike, she couldn't dress too nicely, but she put on one of her favorite brightly colored blouses with long, black shorts and a black blazer. She slipped her feet into flat black espadrilles and put a few things in her bag. Lisa had already fallen back asleep by the time she left the cabin.

When she finally got to Ryan's, which was a few miles from camp, Nicole was starving. She was ready for the biggest breakfast the restaurant had to offer. After parking her bicycle, she walked into the old country-style restaurant. Ryan's had been around since the 1940s, and it showed. There was a long, old-fashioned soda fountain and booths along the windows. The surfaces of most of the tables had been carved with so many initials that they were jagged. Small, red-checked place mats covered the rough spots.

Nicole walked past the first few booths toward one in the back for some privacy. She planned to draw up a list of reasons why she needed to leave camp immediately. She'd have to come up with something a little more drastic sounding than "the food's terrible" or "I hate my cabin."

"Nicole!" someone called out. She turned around. Eliot Packard was sitting in a booth with an older man, who had to be his father. "Come on over and have breakfast with us," Eliot said.

"I don't want to intrude," she said.

"You won't be intruding," Eliot said. He smiled at her, and she was struck by how handsome he looked, especially considering the fact that it was so early in the morning. His blue eyes lit up when he smiled, and he looked as if he was genuinely happy to see her, which was a surprise.

Nicole shrugged. "Well, okay." She wouldn't mind Eliot's company, and his father might turn out to be interesting.

"Nicole Talbot, this is my father, Steven Packard." Eliot's father stood up and shook Nicole's outstretched hand.

"It's a pleasure to meet you, Nicole," he said. "Please, have a seat."

*Finally—someone with some manners!* Nicole thought, sliding into the booth beside Eliot.

"Nicole's a JC, too," Eliot said. "She's from Manhattan."

"No kidding! And how are you surviving your summer in the wilderness? Isn't it great to get away from the heat and dirt of the city? Boy, I just love it up here," Mr. Packard said.

Nicole felt her heart sink. She thought she was going to find someone who might sympathize with her, not a nature lover. She would much rather talk about the city than about boring old Middlebrook. "It's okay, I guess. There's not much to do up here, though."

"Really? Eliot gave me the impression that you were busy all the time," Mr. Packard replied. "Don't they make you counselors work hard?"

"Definitely," Nicole agreed. "But we do the same thing every day. There's no variety."

"Yeah, the routine gets a little boring sometimes,"

Eliot added. "Especially the getting-up-at-six-thirty part."

"Six thirty? Are you crazy? I get up at seven fifteen," Nicole said.

"How come you always look so put together when you show up at flagpole, then?" Eliot asked. "Nicole's the best dresser at camp," he told his father.

Nicole felt her face turn slightly pink. It had been a long time since anyone had complimented her. "Practice," she said. "I have it down to a science."

"I guess." Eliot laughed. "Actually, I get up early so I can go for a walk and listen to some music on my Walkman before the day starts. That's one thing I really miss about home—being able to listen to whatever I want, whenever I want."

"Me, too. That and about a hundred other things." Nicole smiled wanly at Eliot.

"Nicole, what would you like to eat?" Mr. Packard asked as the waitress approached. "We've already ordered."

Nicole recognized the woman from earlier trips to Ryan's, and she smiled at her. "Hi, I'd like two eggs scrambled, with bacon, and pancakes," she said. "And coffee."

The waitress nodded. "Your orders will be right out."

"The great thing about being in Vermont is that you get real maple syrup for free," Eliot said. "You know, Nicole, I don't think I've ever seen you eat as

42

much as you just ordered. This is going to be interesting."

"Well, it's our day off, so I decided to live it up,"
Nicole joked.

"Dad forgot to bring the bagels, so we ended up
here instead," Eliot said.

"You must have gotten in last night," Nicole said
to Mr. Packard.

"Yes. I spent the night at a charming little inn,
right here in town," Mr. Packard said.

Nicole raised one eyebrow. The Middlebrook Inn
—charming? She decided it must be a matter of per-
spective. If she were just visiting town, she might
find it all very pretty and charming—she *might*, that
is, if she knew she was leaving by nightfall.

"So what are you up to today?" Eliot asked, smiling.

"Nothing much," Nicole said. "I'll probably write
some letters, call some friends—just take it easy.
What about you?"

"I'm going to take Dad sailing, then this afternoon
we're going rafting down the Cody River," Eliot
said. "If you want to come along—"

"No, that's okay," Nicole said. "Thanks." She'd
expected Eliot to say they were going somewhere
interesting. She was even hoping they could give her
a ride somewhere, or that she could join them for a
movie. If sailing and rafting were Eliot's idea of a
day off, then maybe they didn't have as much in
common as she thought.

"It's going to feel wonderful to be out on the water," Mr. Packard said as the waitress set down plates of food on the table. "Driving over the East River doesn't really count, you know."

Nicole laughed.

"So where do you live in the city?" Eliot asked, digging into an omelette.

"Upper East Side," Nicole said. She sipped her coffee.

"We live on the Upper West Side," Mr. Packard said. "Riverside Drive."

"It's pretty nice, if you can stand dealing with those stuffy doormen," Eliot added. "And passing about five security checkpoints to get into the building."

Nicole laughed, but just hearing him talk about his apartment building made her feel homesick. She couldn't wait to call her mother.

*Soon,* she thought, swallowing her first bite of pancakes. *Soon I'll be somewhere where I can eat whatever I want—and it won't be hot dogs!*

"Mother! I've been trying to reach you all day!" Nicole was using the only pay phone at camp, in the Lodge. It was just before dinner on Saturday, when they officially went back on duty. "Where have you been?"

"Out, I suppose. What's wrong? You sound upset," her mother said.

"I am," Nicole said. "Mother, you've got to get me out of this camp."

Her mother sighed. "Now, Nicole, we're not going to go through this again, are we?"

"Mother, you do *not* understand how horrible it is here. May I just tell you what happened to me the other day? One of the other junior counselors, who happens to live in the same cabin that I do, put a huge *worm* in my overnight bag." Nicole paused, waiting for her mother to react. "I mean, isn't that the most juvenile thing you've ever heard of?"

"Are you sure one of your campers didn't do it?" asked Mrs. Talbot. She laughed lightly. "I remember doing something like that to a girl when I was in school. She screamed so loudly, you could hear it all the way across the playground."

Nicole tapped her fingernails against the wall. So much for getting any sympathy from dear old Mom. "Well, it was pretty disgusting," she said. "Anyway, that's not even the half of it. I got marshmallow in my hair, then Mara yelled at me for missing lunch and made me mop the kitchen floor. Do you know that we're actually expected to compete in tugs-of-war and three-legged races when the stupid Camp Comps start?"

"Nicole, darling, what did you expect? You're at camp," her mother said.

*I didn't expect to be shipped off here for the summer!* Nicole thought angrily. It wasn't fair that her parents could make up their minds for her. She was seventeen, practically an adult. Her mother obviously wasn't going to listen to any of her real reasons for wanting to leave. It was time to think of something else. "Mother, there's something I haven't told you. I've—"

"Listen, darling, I'd love to talk, but I really am on my way out the door," her mother interrupted. "I'm meeting a friend for dinner in a few minutes, and I don't want to be late."

A friend? Nicole knew what that meant. Whenever her mother said "a friend," what she really meant was the "new man in her life." "How's your back?" she asked, practically fuming. Supposedly the main reason Nicole had had to go to camp was that her mother had run off to Arizona to get her back fixed. Now here she was having a big summer romance!

"It's coming along. My massage therapist thinks it'll only be a few more weeks."

"That's nice." Nicole twirled the phone cord around her index finger. She was angry with her mother for not listening to her, but she couldn't exactly *stay* angry if she wanted her mother to come rescue her. "Do you have Daddy's phone number in France, by any chance?" she asked.

"No, I don't. I think you can call his Connecticut number and leave a message, though. Now I really have to run—take care of yourself, and don't be so down. The summer's already half over!" her mother said.

*Was that supposed to cheer me up?* Nicole wondered as she hung up the phone. The summer was half over, and in her opinion, she'd already wasted half of it at Kissamee. She didn't intend to waste the second half being miserable.

She trudged back down the hall into the dining room, which was almost full, and wandered over to her cabin's table. "Nicole, we missed you today," said Katy Wolff, the CIT for Girls' Thirteen.

"Yeah, what did you do?" asked Mimi.

"Not much." Nicole slid into a chair. "There's not a whole lot to do in town, in case you haven't noticed."

"How come your parents didn't visit?" Zoe asked, passing a big bowl of salad down the table.

Nicole shrugged. *Because they don't care.* "They're too far away," she said. "My mother's in Arizona, and my father's in France."

"Wow! Cool!" said Janet, helping herself to a roll from the basket. Saturday-night dinners, as a rule, were much better than the ones during the rest of the week, but Nicole wasn't hungry. It wasn't because of the big breakfast she'd eaten, either. She hadn't felt this bad since her parents' divorce.

*I'll call Daddy later,* she decided. Her father had come to her rescue before. Maybe he did want her to spend the summer here, but after he heard how truly unhappy she was, he'd have to change his mind.

"So, is everyone psyched about the Comps?" Katy asked.

"What happens if we're all on different teams?" Mimi asked. She looked down the table at Zoe, Marian, and Janet.

"We'll just beat you, that's all," Janet replied, looking smug.

"I hope I get to be on Andy Brenner's team," Marian said, gazing across the dining room.

"Marian's in *love*," Casey Koller teased.

"Dee, what happens if everyone in the cabin is on opposite teams?" Katy asked. "Won't that create a lot of tension?"

"Oh, come on, this isn't the Olympics," Nicole said. "It won't be that competitive."

"I wouldn't be so sure," Katy said. She leaned closer to Nicole. "I read in a book that competition is very important to thirteen-year-olds. In fact, they have a real need to prove themselves as they enter the teenage years."

Nicole shook her head. Katy had spent the winter reading up on child psychology in order to prepare herself for her CIT job. At first, Nicole had found some of the things Katy said helpful. But at this point, she was pretty tired of hearing Dr. Katy's opinion on how to deal with kids. She cast a hopeful glance at Dee, who had been uncharacteristically quiet. "Dee, is this thing really as big a deal as everyone says?"

Dee was staring straight ahead, with a funny expression on her face.

"Dee?" Katy asked.

"I don't feel . . . so good," Dee finally said. The color on her face suddenly turned from pale white, to pink, then back again.

"No offense, but you don't look so good, either. Maybe you'd better go to the infirmary," Nicole said.

"Or at least go back to the cabin and lie down," Katy said.

Dee nodded. "I think I will." She pushed away her plate of uneaten food. "Excuse me." Then she got up from the table and hurried out of the dining room.

"She looks terrible," Katy said. "I hope she's not too sick. Something like that could really spread through the cabin. The last thing we need is ten sick campers."

"No kidding," Nicole said. Although the way her summer was going, she wouldn't be surprised if *she* got sick, too. Of course, she wouldn't get sick enough to leave—no, she'd just end up feeling physically awful on top of being depressed and miserable.

Nicole knew she was feeling sorry for herself, but she couldn't help it. She'd never forgive her parents for sending her away for the summer. Never.

"I think it must have been something I ate," Jennifer said. She was lying on the top bunk bed rubbing her stomach. Her forehead was hot, and she was sweating.

"Jen, I know Wally's not a good cook, but I think it's a little more serious than that." Annie peered up at her. "You should go to the infirmary."

Jennifer groaned. "I hate going there."

"Oh, come on. It's not so bad. If we both hadn't been there when we were eight, we never would have met and become such good friends," Annie reminded her.

"Are you telling me I should go to the infirmary to meet people?" Jennifer asked. "I'm not really in the mood to be social." She rolled over onto her side and curled up in a ball.

"That's it—you're going," Annie said.

She helped Jennifer down, then packed a pair of flannel pajamas and a few books into a bag. They were on their way out the door of the Shack when Nicole walked in.

"Now I really feel sick," Jennifer said.

Nicole looked concerned. "Are you sick, too?" she asked.

"Yeah, she has a fever, chills, stomachache—probably some sort of stomach bug," Annie said. "I'm taking her to the infirmary."

"Good," Nicole said, nodding.

"Gee, thanks for the sympathy," Jennifer said.

"I didn't mean it that way," Nicole said. "It's just —well, Dee is sick, too. I think she might be going over there. Neither of you looks very good."

"Thanks again," Jennifer said. "I didn't have time to put on any make-up because I was sick to my stomach."

Nicole made a face. "Please, spare me the details. All I meant was, it's good if you go there before everyone else in here gets sick."

"Nicole's right—if we all get sick, there won't be anybody to take care of the campers," Annie said. "Now, before you get any sicker, let's go."

"I hope you feel better," Nicole said as Jennifer walked past her, holding on to Annie for support.

"You're just worried about catching it from me," Jennifer said. "Well, don't worry—I didn't breathe in your part of the Shack." As soon as the words were out of her mouth, Jennifer regretted them. Maybe Nicole was being sincere. She seemed to be genuinely concerned, and when Jennifer suggested she wasn't, she looked incredibly hurt. For the first time that Jennifer could remember, Nicole didn't attempt a stinging comeback.

Then a sharp pain shot through her stomach, and she grasped Annie's arm a little tighter. "Come on, let's go," she said.

*Worrying about Nicole? I must be delirious,* she thought.

# CHAPTER
## FIVE

When Nicole woke up the next morning, she felt fine—until she heard the loud clap of thunder. "Oh, no," she groaned, rolling over and putting a pillow over her head. "Just what we need, a storm."

Lisa was humming to herself as she got dressed. "I think it's cozy," she said, running a brush through her reddish-brown hair. "Besides, we'll be able to play some indoor games if this keeps up."

"If this keeps up, Camp Kissamee will probably wash away," Nicole said, sitting up in bed. "Not that that would be such a horrible thing," she added under her breath.

"I hope I can do something with Michael's cabin today," Lisa said. "I didn't see him at *all* yesterday."

Nicole glanced across the room at Lisa, who was trying out combs in her hair, oblivious to the world. For a brief instant she actually wished she were Lisa. Her roommate was in love, and she looked so happy.

*I must really be losing it,* Nicole told herself, reaching for her robe. *If I start wanting to be Lisa*

*Siegel, plain old Lisa Siegel, then things must be even worse than I thought!*

At that moment, the back door to the Shack opened, and Mara Nye walked into the room. "Oh, good. You're up." She shook the water off her yellow slicker.

Nicole stood up and wrapped her robe around her body.

"What is it?" asked Lisa. "Is something wrong?"

"Well, it looks as though we might have a little viral epidemic on our hands. Besides Jennifer, Dee has it, and so do a few of the girls from Jen's cabin. They're all in the infirmary, though, and I think we'll be able to contain it. I'm surprised you're still feeling all right, Nicole," Mara said.

"Me? Why wouldn't I?" asked Nicole.

"Well, you were on that overnight, too. So far most of the victims came down with it after that fishing trip," Mara said.

"Maybe they ate some bad fish," Nicole said. "I didn't have any."

Mara shook her head. "It's definitely a virus, not food poisoning. Anyway, that's why I'm here. Nicole, you'll need to get some things to bring over to Girls' Thirteen."

"What?" Nicole couldn't believe what she'd just heard.

"You'll be staying with the cabin until Dee is healthy enough to come back," Mara said. "Probably three or four nights."

"But—I won't get any sleep," Nicole protested.

Mara grinned. "Think of it this way: It'll be good training for being a full counselor next year."

"Right," Nicole said with a curt nod. As if she were planning on coming back!

"Get dressed, and I'll walk over there with you," Mara said. "If the girls hear it from me that you'll be staying with them, they'll probably treat you a little better. Besides, you need to take them to flagpole."

"Don't tell me we have to stand outside in this weather," Nicole said. "We'll all come down with the flu."

Lisa laughed. "No, it's in the Lodge on rainy days, remember?"

"Come on, Nicole, let's go," Mara said.

"Right now? But I need to take a shower, and—"

"There isn't time for all that," Mara said. "Just put on some clothes, pack a few things, and be ready in ten minutes. I'm going over to Brett's cabin to see if anyone there feels ill. I'll swing by here on my way back."

"Great," Nicole said as the screen door slammed shut behind Mara. "There's a hurricane outside, and I'm going to live in a cabin with ten thirteen-year-olds."

"You get along with them, though, don't you?" Lisa asked. "Isn't there one you like in particular?"

Nicole thought about Mimi. At least she wouldn't terrorize everyone else while Dee was gone. As for

54

the rest of them . . . "I feel like quitting right now!" she said, marching into the bathroom.

"It's not that bad," Lisa said. "The rain will probably stop by tomorrow."

*And by tomorrow I want to be out of here,* Nicole said to herself as she brushed her teeth. Maybe tomorrow was unrealistic, but by the end of the week, she would be gone. She wasn't going to tell anyone about her plan—especially not Lisa, who'd try to talk her out of it. She wasn't exactly sure of it, yet, but if her father wouldn't send for her, she'd arrange her own departure—one way or another.

"Girls, I have an announcement to make!" Mara called out. Nicole, standing behind her, didn't see why she needed to shout. The cabin wasn't much bigger than the Shack. "Since Dee will be holed up in the infirmary for the next few days, Nicole is going to move in—"

"All right, Nicole!" Zoe yelled, giving her the thumbs-up signal.

Mara frowned at her. "As I was saying, Nicole will stay here and look after you. If you have any problems, please don't hesitate to tell her about them."

"Nicole, Marian has a problem," Janet said. "She's in love with a counselor!"

Marian hit her on the arm. "Cut it out!"

Nicole felt a headache coming on. She couldn't put up with this shrieking much longer. Spending even one night with the same girls who'd put itching powder in her sleeping bag was going to be torture, pure torture.

"Quiet down, girls. I hope you'll all be on your best behavior for Nicole. Remember, you've already been in trouble once this summer for the raid on Boys' Thirteen." Zoe whistled, and a few of the girls giggled. Mara cleared her throat. "Please don't make this any harder for Nicole. I'll be watching you."

She patted Nicole on the arm, and raindrops dribbled from her hand. "I'll be watching you, too, Nicole. You'll need to be extra careful. But don't worry," she added. "I'm sure they'll be perfectly fine. Oh, and don't forget, you have inspection tomorrow morning." Before she went out the door she cast a parting look at the cabin, which was in a shambles. "I'm sure Nicole will help you make this place look respectable by then."

*Yeah, right,* Nicole thought as Mara hurled herself back into the lashing rain. She turned to face her campers. "Okay, guys. You heard what Mara said. Let's get this place cleaned up."

She looked around the cabin and felt her headache start to pound. As bad as the Shack was, at least it was a refuge from real camp life, which now struck Nicole in all its horror. The ten girls in the cabin had covered every available inch of wall space with posters of rock stars and TV actors. Clothing was strewn everywhere, poking out of drawers, heaped up in piles on the floor. It was hard to find a single spot in the cabin that wasn't trashed. Nicole glanced into the bathroom. She'd never noticed how bad it was before because she hadn't had to worry about it—*she* didn't live here. Bottles and jars of shampoo, make-up, lotion, and sunblock were piled all over the place, half of them open and oozing out onto the floor.

"How can you guys live like this?" Nicole cried.

"Puh-lease, you sound like my mother," Zoe said.

"We don't have time to clean," Janet said. "We have to go to flagpole in ten minutes."

"Where's Katy?" asked Nicole, gritting her teeth. Although Nicole hadn't paid much attention to Katy in the past, she suddenly realized how much she was going to need her to deal with this group.

"She went to see Dee," Mimi said. "She said she'd be back to get us for flagpole."

"What are we going to *do* today?" Betsy looked out the window by her bunk bed.

"Maybe we could go surfing on Torch Lake," Marian said. "The way the wind's blowing, I bet there will even be waves."

"What about the Comps? Are they going to be called off?" asked Janet.

Nicole felt as if a hundred voices were coming at her at once. "It'll probably clear up by tomorrow," she said. "Today I think they've planned rainy-day stuff in the Lodge."

"I heard it was going to storm all week," Lynne Diamond said. "I hate it when it rains. We can't do anything—no horseback riding, no sailing, nothing."

"Hanging out in the Lodge? What a total drag," Zoe said. "Can't we at least go somewhere fun?"

Nicole had to agree with Zoe on that. A rainy day would be much more tolerable if she could spend it at a mall or a museum. "This is a big storm. I don't think anyone's going anywhere today," she said. "It might be dangerous to travel."

The cabin door swung open, and Katy came in, completely drenched. "It's unbelievable out there!" she said. "I've never seen such wild weather here."

"Do we *have* to go over to the Lodge for flag-pole?" asked Janet.

"Yes, we do," Nicole said. "Katy, which one is Dee's bed?"

Katy pointed to a bunk bed by one of the windows. "She sleeps on the bottom, underneath me. Why, are you staying here now?" Nicole nodded. "Great!" Katy said enthusiastically. "It'll give us a chance to get to know each other, and you'll be able to see some real camper interaction."

Katy had the uncanny ability to make everything sound like a psychology experiment. Actually, Katy might learn something by studying Nicole over the next few days: If she didn't lose her mind, it would be a major miracle!

Jennifer kept trying to take a sip from the glass of water next to her bed, but every time she sat up, she felt as if she were going to faint. She couldn't remember the last time she had felt so sick. She kept

58

getting the chills, and then five minutes later she'd be burning up.

She could hear voices in the hallway, and then a moment later, the door to her room opened. "I told you, we're trying to quarantine them so it doesn't spread," the nurse said.

"All I want to do is deliver these," a familiar voice replied. Jennifer looked up and saw Josh standing at the end of the bed, holding a bouquet of wildflowers.

"Jennifer, I'm sorry you're not feeling well," he said, handing the flowers to her. Jennifer was almost too weak to lift her arm to take them from him. "Wow, you're really shaky," Josh said. "Here, I'll put them"—he glanced around and found a glass of water—"right here. So how are you?"

Jennifer shrugged, feeling woozy. "Pretty lousy."

"Josh, you really should go now. She's highly contagious," the nurse warned.

"Okay, okay. Hang in there, Jen. I'll come back and visit you. Get lots of sleep!" Josh called as the nurse ushered him out the door.

Jennifer waved feebly, then turned over. She wasn't sure how long she had been asleep when there was a knock at the door, and Annie walked in. Nurse Barnes was right behind her. "Annie, you really shouldn't—"

"I know, I know," Annie said. "I just wanted to bring her something." She took a small teddy bear from underneath her rain poncho and put it beside Jennifer. "I borrowed it from a girl in my cabin who said she's getting too old for it. She'll probably want it back soon, but you should be out of here by then," Annie said.

Jennifer smiled. "Thanks."

"Wow, what nice flowers! Where did those come from? Your cabin?" asked Annie.

"No. Josh," Jennifer said.

"Really? Are you guys good friends now or something?"

"No. Well, maybe." Jennifer finally managed to take a sip of water. She was going through one of her burning-up stages.

"Bringing you flowers? I don't know, that sounds like something else," Annie said.

Jennifer didn't know if it was her fever or what, but Annie wasn't making any sense to her. "Like what?"

"Like maybe he has a crush on you!" Annie whispered. Nurse Barnes was still standing at the door, watching them closely.

"That's crazy," Jennifer said. "He just brought them because I'm sick."

Annie raised one eyebrow. "I didn't see any in Dee's room when I stopped by to bring her a card we all made for her in arts and crafts."

"Annie, please," Nurse Barnes said. "If you're not careful, you'll get sick, too. You can see how miserable Jennifer is."

Annie took a few steps backward. "I'll see you later, Jen. I hope you feel better soon."

60

A shiver ran through Jennifer's body, and she pulled the sheets up around her neck. She hugged the teddy bear to her chest. What was Annie talking about? She wasn't even sure Josh had brought those flowers—it seemed like a dream to her. Anyway, he didn't like her any more than he liked Annie, or Dee, or anyone else. He was just being nice.

"So, how's it going over at Girls' Thirteen?" Lisa asked. She and Nicole were sitting at a table in the Lodge waiting for a game of charades to get started between their cabins. It was late Sunday afternoon, and Nicole had been cooped up in the Lodge all day with her campers, playing various games. The kids from each cabin were rotating around the room, going from one game to the next. Wally was preparing the cookout meal as planned, but he was using the kitchen ovens instead of cooking outdoors. The smell of barbecued chicken was practically making Nicole's mouth water, and there was still an hour to wait before dinner.

"It's okay, so far," Nicole said. "I bet tonight will be the worst. We have to clean the cabin for inspection, and I know no one wants to—including me."

"Maybe it won't be too bad," Lisa said. "At least then you'll have a nice place to live."

"Yeah, for a few seconds," Nicole said.

"Nicole, will you buy me a soda?" Janet asked.

"Me, too!" said Zoe.

"Me, three!" added Marian.

"Do you guys have to do *everything* together?" Nicole snapped.

"Actually, they're quite dependent on each other," Katy, who was sitting on the other side of Nicole, whispered. "And that creates a strange dynamic in the cabin, because they tend to lead, while everyone else follows."

Nicole stared at her. "Katy, all they did was ask for a soda at the same time."

"Yes, but it shows how they need to be connected to each other." Katy pointed to some of the other girls in the cabin. "Now they're not nearly so dependent, yet they always look to the other three before they do anything."

"Whatever," Nicole said. The whole subject of child psychology bored her. She'd been to a psychiatrist when her parents were divorced—they'd made her go, of course—but she had only lasted a few sessions. It was boring to sit around and talk about her parents.

"So can we get sodas?" Zoe asked.

"I don't think so," Nicole said. She turned to Katy. "Dee doesn't usually buy them sodas, does she?" She had no idea if she was doing the right thing. Half of her wanted to give them sodas so they'd leave her alone, but the other half wanted them to learn that they couldn't have everything they wanted, just like that.

"Sure she does!" Janet said. "Every afternoon."

"She's making it up," Katy said. "Lying. A classic way to get attention, you know."

Of all the luck! Nicole was stuck inside on a rainy day with Dr. Freud.

"So, are you guys ready to play?" asked Lisa. She and her cabin of eleven-year-olds had been having a conference about what charade to do first. The head counselor, Nancy McDowell, was there, too, and Nicole briefly considered asking her to help out over at Girls' Thirteen. She and Lisa could look after the eleven-year-olds together. Lisa liked to work—and besides, she was better with kids than Nicole was. But Nicole didn't want anybody to think that she couldn't handle a cabin on her own. She could. She just didn't *want* to.

A girl in Lisa's cabin started to sound out the first clue, and Nicole sighed. She didn't know which was worse—fishing or playing charades. She hadn't even had time to call her father's Connecticut number yet, she'd been so busy running around after everyone all day. That meant her hopes for leaving had to be put off another day. But she hadn't given up. She wasn't going to, until she was on a plane, headed back to New York, over to Paris—anywhere, just as long as it was a one-way ticket out of Vermont.

# CHAPTER
## SIX

"So what team are you on?" Eliot asked Nicole. They had just finished dinner Sunday night, and Brett and Mara had handed out lists to everyone. Because the wind was still howling and the rain hadn't let up, Tim and Cathy had decided to hold an impromptu dance at the Lodge. All the counselors were clearing an open space in the dining room.

"The gray one," Nicole said. "Not that I care."

"I'm blue." Eliot picked up two chairs and moved them off to the side of the room. "You know, it really isn't as bad as you think. It's actually a lot of fun."

"I'll believe it when I see it," Nicole said, dragging a chair behind her.

Eliot followed her. "Why do you have such a bad attitude about everything?"

"Excuse me?" Nicole said.

"Ever since you got here, you've been acting as though you hate everything. It's as if you're determined to have a bad time, and nothing's going to change that," Eliot said.

Nicole whirled around to face him, her face turning pink. "Look, it wasn't my idea to come to this camp. And it just so happens that I *am* having a rotten time." She couldn't believe that Eliot, of all people, couldn't see why she would be unhappy. He at least had some idea of the kind of life she was used to. She'd thought they had been getting along fairly well, too.

"I'm not saying this is the be-all and end-all of existence, but it happens to be a great place to spend the summer, if you'd just start trying to enjoy it." Eliot put two chairs on top of a stack by one of the big picture windows.

Nicole pointed out the window, which was covered with water and pine needles that had been whipped through the air. It was raining so hard that she couldn't even see across the lawn to the arts-and-crafts building. "Tell me how I'm supposed to enjoy this!"

"Oh, so now the weather's responsible for your bad time, too?" Eliot said. "You really expect a lot of a place, don't you?"

Nicole felt the headache she'd had that morning start to come back full force. Who was Eliot to talk to her this way, anyway? She'd thought he was a friend, or at least that he could become one. Where did he get off criticizing her? "I expect people to treat me decently," she said, trying to control her voice.

"That's a two-way street," Eliot said. "I mean, you have to try to get along with people, too."

"Look, Eliot, I don't know whether you've just spent too much time inside today or what, but I really don't need your advice on how to live my life," Nicole retorted.

"I'm not trying to—oh, never mind," Eliot said, staring out the window. "I just thought, maybe if you wanted to talk about it—"

"About what?" demanded Nicole.

"Why you hate it here so much," Eliot said. "It's obvious to me, and to everybody, that you haven't even given it a chance."

Nicole thought about that for a minute. She had stayed at camp for a whole month. Didn't that qualify as giving it a chance? Anyway, why should she? How many times did she have to tell people that this hadn't been her idea? She'd been forced into it by her parents, and she wasn't going to pretend she was having fun when she wasn't.

"Look, Nicole, I'm not trying to start an argument. I just wanted to see if there was anything I could do to make you happier here," Eliot said.

Nicole was surprised by the tone of his voice. He sounded as if he was actually concerned about her. But just a minute ago, he'd been doing nothing but criticizing her. "Yes, there is something you could do," she said, in a phony, pleasant voice. "You could get me out of here, right away!" Then she marched out of the main room and down a narrow corridor to the pay phone. She wasn't supposed to use it as frequently as she had been, but the way she looked at it, this was an *emergency*.

*It figures that a dump like this would only have one phone,* Nicole thought angrily. She was fuming inside at the suggestions Eliot had made. He'd sounded as if he was trying to be *her* counselor. She wasn't a camper, and she didn't need his advice!

She picked up the phone and punched in her father's number in Connecticut. She was surprised the phones were still working in the storm, but extremely grateful. "Collect, from Nicole," she said when the operator came on the line. The phone rang four times before the answering machine picked it up.

"I'm sorry," the operator said. "No answer."

"Daddy? Are you there?" Nicole asked when the message was over.

"We have to cut off the line now since I have no authorization to pay for this call," the operator said.

Click. The line went dead. Nicole rested her head in her hands. Her father must be in Europe already. She felt as if she was going to burst out crying. *Don't cry*, she told herself, taking a deep breath. *Whatever you do, don't cry.*

She stood up and walked back down the hall into the main room. Music was playing, and a few of the campers were dancing. Most of the boys were on one side of the room, and the girls were on the other.

"Nicole, how are the girls in your cabin doing?" Mara asked, coming up beside her.

"Pretty well, I guess, considering the circumstances," Nicole said. "Is this rain ever going to end?"

"Oh, of course it'll end." Mara patted her on the back cheerfully. "But you'll still need to stay at the cabin. I just got a call from the infirmary, and they said it'll probably be three or four days before anyone's better. Which leaves me with another problem —I need to find someone to staff a few positions. I suppose Annie can run arts and crafts by herself, but we will need someone to replace Jennifer down on the waterfront."

"I'll do it," Nicole said immediately. If she was going to be stuck at camp for another week, she might as well hang out down at the lake instead of hauling bows and arrows to the meadow.

"You will?" asked Mara. "Wow, Nicole, I've never seen you volunteer for something so quickly before."

"I like lifeguarding," Nicole said. She hadn't done much of it, but she had enjoyed the courses she took to become certified. "And I could use a break from meadow activities and archery." In the back of her mind was the thought that she just might be able to take Jennifer's job away from her, too. That would really get to her. Jennifer loved working at the waterfront with Andy, one of her best friends at camp. It would kill her if she got discharged from the infirmary and found out that *Nicole* had her job.

68

"But then we'll need to find someone to replace you." Mara tapped her finger against her chin. "I suppose I could take over there—for a few days, anyway."

A smile spread across Nicole's face for the first time all day. "Great!"

"Report to the waterfront, then, tomorrow afternoon. Justin will brief you on your responsibilities," Mara said. Justin O'Connell was the head counselor for waterfront activities. "Thanks, Nicole. I need to go talk to Cathy. And don't forget about inspection tomorrow morning!"

Nicole looked across the room. Annie and Gil were dancing together. Gil was smiling, his face lit up with happiness. Behind them were Lisa and Michael. Michael had probably just told a joke, because Lisa was laughing. She met Eliot's eyes as she surveyed the room for the girls in her cabin, then quickly looked away. Why was he bugging her so much, watching her every move?

"Hey, Mimi," she said as the younger girl approached her. "Why aren't you dancing?"

Mimi shrugged. "I don't feel like it."

"Neither do I," said Nicole. "Where's everyone else?"

"Over there." Mimi pointed to a close circle of girls by one of the large couches.

Nicole sympathized with Mimi. She could see that it must not be easy to be shy in a cabin that was virtually run by Zoe, Marian, and Janet. She knew what it felt like to be on the outside, too. She'd never really experienced it before—usually she was one of the "in" crowd. But at camp, she was definitely an outsider. It was a strange feeling. Most of the time she didn't even *want* to be friends with the other junior counselors, but she didn't like not being their friend, either.

"How about some punch?" Nicole asked Mimi. Mimi nodded, and together they walked over to the buffet table. "So what team are you on, Mimi?"

"Gray," said Mimi.

"Are you excited about the games?" asked Nicole, helping herself to a cup of punch and a sugar cookie.

"Kind of," Mimi said. "Some of them sound really fun. I just hope it stops raining so we can start them."

"Me, too," said Nicole. "Me, too." Supervising the cabin was going to be hard enough without everyone being cooped up inside. What if they *all* came down the flu? It was bad enough being a live-in counselor —but a nurse, too?

"*Yuuuuuccccckk!*" Marian's shriek of disgust pierced the stuffy air in Girls' Thirteen. She was hopping around on one foot, her other foot covered with toothpaste. "Who put the toothpaste in my slippers?" she cried.

No one answered—everyone was laughing too hard. "Hey, Marian, that looks like an event for the Comps!" Zoe yelled in between giggles.

"The Toothpaste Hop," Lynne added, clutching her stomach.

Nicole had forgotten how rowdy thirteen-year-old girls could be, but it was all coming back to her on her first night in the cabin. So far she'd had to deal with a short-sheeted bed, a rubber bug under someone's pillow, and a missing cassette tape that Zoe had stolen because Casey was listening to it all the time. She wasn't looking forward to getting into bed and finding out if they had any leftover itching powder.

"Okay, guys, calm down," Nicole said. "We need to clean up this cabin before everyone goes to sleep. Inspection is right after breakfast, remember?"

"We'll do it in the morning," Janet said. "If we do it now it'll just be dirty again by then, anyway."

"Look, do you want to fail inspection? You'll have to clean the stables again, the way you did after your raid," Nicole told them.

"Mara never makes the same cabin clean stables twice in one summer," Zoe said, unruffled.

Nicole glared at her. "There's always a first time, isn't there?"

"You know what?" Katy said, pulling Nicole aside. "I think the loss of their traditional authority figure is causing them to act out. If we could make it clear that the routine is still the same, give them a feeling of consistency . . ."

"What do you suggest?" asked Nicole, her arms folded across her chest. She didn't believe that a fifteen-year-old CIT was going to have any ideas that she hadn't already considered.

"We could make it into a game, or a contest," Katy said. "I know! We could say that it's part of the Comps and separate them into teams."

"They do seem to be ready for some competition," Nicole said. She'd never seen so much pent-up energy in one room before. For the first time, Nicole understood the term "cabin fever." She even thought it might be a good idea to make everyone go for a jog before bed so they'd be too tired to do anything but sleep. "Okay, let's try it." She clapped her hands together. "Katy just reminded me of something. Brett told us today that each cabin can have its own Comps, and one of the events is cabin cleaning. So you guys need to separate into teams. Katy and I will judge who cleans the most, the fastest, and give them the most points. It'll count a lot for your team," she added.

"Are you serious?" asked Marian, wiping her foot with a towel. "This is really part of Comps?"

Nicole and Katy both nodded. "All the cabins are going to be doing it," Nicole lied.

"We'll report the results to Brett tomorrow morning," Katy added.

"Okay, who's on blue?" Zoe yelled.

Half an hour later, the cabin was spotless. Miraculously, all the girls got into bed after arguing about who had really won, and they seemed ready to sleep.

A few were reading, and others were writing letters or talking quietly.

"You're pretty good at this stuff," Nicole said to Katy.

"It's all behavioral psychology. As Skinner would say—"

"Spare me," Nicole said. "Unless this Skinner guy has some ideas about how to stop it from raining tomorrow."

"Don't worry, Nicole—we'll think of something to do! Anyway, Tim and Cathy always have a bunch of stuff planned for rainy days," Katy said cheerfully.

Nicole didn't know if she could stand another day of charades, cards, and word games. Of course, if the rain stopped they would start Comps, which wouldn't be any better. There was only one option, as far as she was concerned: evacuation!

Monday morning, Nicole was woken up by Katy, who stepped on her toe as she got down from the top bunk. "Ouch!" Nicole mumbled into her pillow.

"Sorry," Katy said. "I was going to wake you up, anyway. Do you know it's already six forty-five?"

Katy went into the bathroom, and Nicole rolled over. She wanted to get as much sleep as possible. The girls had been fairly quiet during the night, but she hadn't felt comfortable sleeping in a strange bed. She'd been afraid that the second she fell asleep they'd play some sort of joke on her. Now that she was finally sleeping well, it was time to get up.

She pulled the blanket from around her ears and groaned. There it was. The sound of rain pounding on the roof.

"Everyone's going to need a little extra encouragement to get out of bed today," Katy said, coming back into the room, dressed and ready to go.

"Including me," Nicole mumbled. She reluctantly threw back the covers and marched into the bathroom. Looking at her reflection in the mirror, Nicole shuddered. There were big dark circles under her eyes, and she had a pimple. Nicole wanted to go back to bed and stay there for at least a week. Instead, she washed her face and brushed her hair. Then she changed into a pair of jeans and an old sweater. She didn't care what she looked like. She was just going to get all wet the second she went out the door, anyway.

"Okay, everybody! Get up!" Nicole said at about ten past seven. She hadn't heard the traditional reveille that was bugled every morning at seven. The bugle was probably full of water.

Nobody moved. "We might have to try the cold-water trick," Katy said. "That's what Dee has to do sometimes."

Nicole pulled back the covers on Zoe's bed. "Come on, Zoe. It's time to get up."

Zoe opened one eye and yanked the covers back from her. "I'm not moving."

"Don't you guys want any breakfast?" Nicole said, hoping the thought of hot food would get them up.

The cabin was sort of cold and damp. "Maybe Wally's making waffles today!"

"He doesn't make waffles," Janet grumbled.

"Yeah, and if he did, they'd taste like sawdust, anyway," Lynne added.

So much for that tactic. She should have known better than to try to tempt them with Wally's food. "The Comps start today!" she said, even though she was pretty sure they'd be rained out. "You can't sleep through those!"

Nobody answered. "What's the cold-water thing?" Nicole finally asked Katy.

"Just go up to each one of them and pretend you're going to sprinkle them with cold water," Katy said. "They'll move pretty fast."

"If this rain keeps up, the roof will probably leak, and we'll *all* wake up that way," Nicole said. Katy laughed, and Nicole smiled. It was nice to have a partner to help out, even if she did quote psychologists all the time.

Nicole filled a glass of water in the bathroom and then stood over Marian, who was on a bottom bunk. "If you don't get up, it's going to start raining inside, too," she threatened.

"No!" Marian jumped out of bed. "Okay, I'll get ready."

Ten minutes later, all the girls filed out the door in identical yellow raincoats. Nicole felt as if she were running a day-care center! Still, there was some small satisfaction in having gotten ten girls to do what she wanted them to do. She just hoped their cooperation would last as long as the bad weather did.

# CHAPTER
## SEVEN

"How are we feeling today?"

Jennifer looked up and saw Nurse Barnes hovering over her, holding a thermometer. Her mouth was so dry she could hardly speak. "*I feel a little better*," she said. She reached for the water glass and took a few gulps.

"Well, you're not missing anything outside," the nurse said. "It's still raining so hard that you can't make it from here to the Lodge without getting drenched. Ready now?" Jennifer nodded, and Nurse Barnes slipped the thermometer into her mouth. Jennifer didn't know why she was bothering—she still had a fever. Why did it matter whether it was 101.8 or 102?

"Here—someone dropped this off for you this morning." Nurse Barnes handed Jennifer an envelope. "I'll be back in a few minutes to check your temperature."

When she was gone, Jennifer opened the envelope. She figured it would be another get-well card from Annie, who'd dropped off three already, even though she'd only been in the infirmary for two nights. She pulled out the card. It was a sappy one, with flowers and loopy handwriting that said, "Please Get Well Soon." Jennifer wondered if this was a joke. She glanced inside—there was a short note, signed by Josh Phillips, of all people.

"Dear Jennifer," she read. "The nurse won't let me come to visit you anymore because she says you need your rest. I hope you're feeling a lot better. I worry about you. And camp is really boring without you. Please hurry up and get well so you can come on the hayride with me. Love, Josh."

"'Love, Josh'?" Jennifer said out loud. She would have swallowed the thermometer if it hadn't been trapped under her tongue. What was going on? Did Josh seriously have a crush on her? Jennifer didn't know what to do. She didn't know Josh well enough to know if she liked him—they'd only spent a little time together, most of it on that overnight a few days ago. Did he really like her? Or was he just being friendly?

"Love, Josh," she read again. Most boys she knew didn't sign their letters like that unless . . .

Nurse Barnes walked into the room and took the thermometer out of her mouth. "Well, it looks as though you're on the road to recovery. You're down to ninety-nine point eight," she said with a smile. "Dee's feeling better, too."

Jennifer wasn't sure if she wanted to get better or not. If she did, she'd have to face Josh—and she had no idea what to say to him. As long as she was quarantined, she could avoid dealing with the whole situation. Jennifer wasn't used to anyone having a crush on her—it was usually the other way around. She didn't know which was worse!

"Some people are going to spend the morning having horse-grooming lessons in the barn, others will head over to arts and crafts, and the rest of us are going to have a board-game extravaganza!" Mara announced cheerfully on Monday morning at a makeshift flagpole meeting. Everyone was sitting inside at their breakfast tables, with water dripping off their jackets and making pools on the floor.

*It figures,* Nicole thought. The one day when she might actually look forward to her afternoon activity, there wasn't going to *be* any.

"Are we ever going to have Comps?" asked Casey.

"Yeah, why can't we start some of the races inside," Lynne added.

"*Shh,*" Nicole told them.

"This will push the Comps back a day, but the weather report on this morning's news said that the rain should taper off sometime tomorrow," Mara continued. "I know it's a disappointment, but we'll still have time to fit everything in. In the meantime, enjoy yourselves!"

Nicole passed a pitcher of orange juice to Mimi, who was sitting on her right.

"Hey, Mimi, did you check the mail yet?" Zoe asked. "Maybe you got a letter this morning."

"Yeah, it's been at least a *day* since the last letter from your mother," Janet added.

Mimi blushed. "I can't help it if she writes me all the time."

"She got three letters from her last week," Zoe informed Nicole.

"Well, how many letters did you get?" Nicole asked her.

Zoe shrugged. "A couple. But not from my mother—from my friends at home."

"You're both luckier than I am!" Nicole said. "I didn't get any mail last week." She was hoping that her complaint would switch everyone's attention from Mimi to her. She could take their teasing, but Mimi had obviously heard enough of it lately.

"Neither did I," said Casey. "My parents have only written me twice this whole summer!"

"That's twice more than mine," Nicole said. "They're too busy, or they say they're not good at writing letters. They have a lot of excuses, but the fact is, they're lazy." The other fact Nicole didn't mention was that sometimes she felt as if her parents didn't care about her enough to write to her. Her mother was usually wrapped up in her own life of spas and boyfriends, and her father put his work before Nicole.

"You should see my dad," Katy said. "He's the original couch potato." Everyone started laughing,

80

and the tension between Mimi and Zoe was broken. Nicole made a mental note to talk to Mimi later and find out how she was doing. She had a feeling Mimi's summer wasn't going any better than hers.

"It can't keep raining, can it?" Nicole asked on Tuesday morning. She had just survived night number two with Girls' Thirteen. The second night hadn't been any easier than the first—by the time everyone went to sleep, it had been at least two o'clock. After another morning of listening to Brett and Mara talk cheerfully about indoor activities, Nicole thought she was going to lose her mind. The girls in Cabin Thirteen weren't far behind.

"Why is Wally's French toast so incredibly bad?" Zoe lifted a corner of the piece on her plate, inspecting the next one underneath.

"At least it's not that horrible oatmeal," Marian commented. "That stuff reminds me of Super Glue."

"I know. The last time I ate it, I couldn't stand to put anything else in my mouth for the rest of the day. I think my *stomach* was stuck together," Casey added.

"How about the lasagna?" Janet asked. "It tastes like the paste I used to eat back in elementary school."

"So that's why you're so strange." Katy grinned.

Janet glared at her. "Yeah, and if I keep eating Wally's food all summer, I'll probably end up totally weird."

81

Nicole smiled. She'd had to eat food this bad before—the year she went to boarding school. Her parents had thought that being away from home might help her "adjust" better to their divorce. *No wonder I don't like being stuck in New England,* Nicole thought. *This isn't the first time.*

Actually, a lot of things about Camp Kissamee reminded her of that year she'd spent at Brentwood Prep: living in close quarters with a bunch of people she didn't know, eating meals with them in the dining hall, having to be somewhere at all times of the day. *Maybe I hate it so much here because it reminds me of the year my parents split up,* Nicole thought.

Then she shook her head and took a sip of fruit juice, brushing the thought away. Obviously, she had been spending too much time with Katy, listening to her pop-psychology theories. *I don't like it here because it's* wretched, *that's all.*

"Well, I don't think the rain is so awful." Marian twisted a strand of light blond hair around her finger. "I think rain makes everything much more romantic."

"Spare us," Janet groaned. "That's all we hear about. Isn't Andy cute? Doesn't Andy have great shoulders? Andy has the best sense of humor, doesn't he?" She mimicked Marian's voice.

"Well, he *does,*" Marian said, not letting Janet's teasing bother her.

"Wait a second," Nicole said. "You don't still have a crush on Andy Brenner, do you?"

"Does it rain in Vermont?" Zoe retorted.

Nicole looked at Marian. "Isn't Andy a little old for you?"

Marian shrugged. "I don't think so. I happen to be really mature for my age. Just ask Katy," she said, turning to the CIT for confirmation. "She did a personality test on me the other day, and I was answering questions like an eighteen-year-old."

Katy frowned. "According to the psychologists who developed this test, you're very grown-up for your age—in some respects. But I never said you were mature enough to go out with a counselor."

"A *junior* counselor," Marian corrected her. "Andy's only seventeen. Anyway, everyone knows that girls grow up faster than boys."

Nicole couldn't help agreeing with that. She had almost never been interested in any boys her age—except Gil. But she still didn't think it was appropriate for a thirteen-year-old girl to date a boy four years older than she. "You really ought to choose someone a little closer to your own age," she told Marian. "Apart from a lot of other problems, you're only going to put Andy on the spot if you flirt with him. Just ask Mara how she feels about campers dating counselors. I'm pretty sure it's not even allowed."

Marian looked crushed. "You mean they wouldn't let us date? They'd try to keep us apart?"

"In a word, yes," Nicole said calmly. She took a

bite of French toast. It actually tasted almost good to her.

"I don't believe this place," Marian muttered. "They can't tell us how to do everything. We have rights, you know."

*Oh, great,* Nicole thought. Now she had a girl who wanted to start a camp protest in her cabin. She glanced out the big picture windows at the rain, which was pouring down with all the consistency of a shower turned on full blast.

Katy leaned over to whisper in Nicole's ear. "She has two older sisters, you know. I think she wants to get Andy's attention because it will make her feel like more of an adult."

Nicole put down her fork and tried not to scream. Between the bad weather, Dee's being sick, Katy's child-psychology lectures, and the girls in her cabin, Nicole was ready to call it quits.

*Not yet,* she told herself, *but soon!* Either she'd convince her mom to come get her, or she'd track down her father—or she'd leave all by herself. But she wasn't going to be sitting at the same table a week from today. She didn't care if she had to paddle a canoe all the way back to New York—she'd get there somehow.

"I should have screened Megan's movie choices, but it never occurred to me that anyone would want to see that corny old movie," Nicole said to Katy that night in the Lodge. Tim and Cathy had arranged for

84

everyone to watch videos on the large-screen TV that a parent had donated to the camp at the beginning of the summer. Megan and her cabin, Girls' Twelve, had gone into Middlebrook to the video store and picked out *West Side Story*. Now it was all Marian could talk about. She kept telling everyone that she and Andy were separated by the cruel forces of society, just like Maria and Tony.

"She's obviously completely identified with Maria," Katy agreed.

"She's telling the whole camp that she and Andy are madly in love, and only Kissamee's harsh rules are keeping Andy from telling her how he feels." Nicole shook her head. "I don't want to break her heart, but the truth is that Andy was infatuated with *me*, not her, and he probably still is."

She looked across the lodge at Andy. Marian was standing a few feet away from him, gazing at him longingly, like a lost puppy. Andy didn't even seem to notice that she was there—he was talking to Gil and some of the boys in his cabin.

"Now what are we going to do?" Mimi asked.

"I guess we'll go back to the cabin," Nicole said with a shrug. "It's getting late." She was about to go look out the window for the millionth time that day, to check on the weather, when Mara walked up to her.

"Nicole, I have some great news!" she said. "First, Tim and Cathy have decided that if it's still raining tomorrow, the whole camp will go to the natural history museum in Woodstock!"

"The natural history museum?" Nicole repeated. It wasn't exactly her idea of a good time, but Woodstock *was* a bigger town. Maybe she'd be able to slip away from the group somehow and hop on a bus south. And if she couldn't, it would still mean getting away from camp for a day. "That sounds great!" she said enthusiastically.

"They've chartered a few buses to drive down first thing in the morning," Mara said. "But that's not even the best news. I stopped by the infirmary to visit Dee a few hours ago, and her fever's all gone. She says she feels terrific, and Dr. Porter said that if it's still down tomorrow morning, she can come back to the cabin! And that means *you're* free to go back to the Shack."

"Really?" Nicole twisted the Swatch on her arm. This was what she had been waiting for—a chance to escape Girls' Thirteen. So why didn't she feel thrilled? She imagined moving her things back into the Shack and sleeping in the bed across from Lisa's. The other JCs had probably gotten even closer since Nicole had been away. They'd probably even shared mean stories about her, laughing at her behind her back.

"Yes, you'll be able to get your life back." Mara smiled.

*Some life,* thought Nicole. The truth was, despite all the problems and headaches, she'd been happier living in Girls' Thirteen than she had been since she'd shown up at camp. *Don't tell me I'm actually becoming* attached *to this place,* Nicole thought, looking across the room at Marian, Zoe, Janet, and Lynne.

"You'll still be our counselor, though, won't you?" asked Mimi.

Nicole smiled at her. "Sure I will. Katy, would you help me collect everyone to go back to the cabin?" she asked. "I have a little surprise for you all."

"What is it?" Mimi asked eagerly.

"Let's just say it's something that'll make everyone feel better," Nicole said. She had arranged for Megan to buy some *real* food for her at the store when she took the camp van into Middlebrook: cookies, chips and dip, and some candy. Nicole didn't mind spending fifteen dollars of her summer allowance on the girls—she thought they deserved it, after having been stuck inside for three straight days. Tonight, they were going to have an old-fashioned pig-out. And from what Nicole could remember, that is one of the favorite activities of thirteen-year-old girls.

*And,* she thought, *this* might *just be my last meal at this place—so it might as well be good!*

# CHAPTER
## EIGHT

"It must feel great to be out of the infirmary," Annie said as she and Jennifer strolled up the wide front steps of the Lodge on Wednesday for lunch. It was a glorious sunny day, and the ground was finally beginning to dry out after all the rain.

"Does it ever," Jennifer replied. She was enjoying the fresh air. "The first day I was there, I was so sick, I didn't even know where I was. Hey, let's go downstairs and check our mail before we eat." They walked through the main room and down the corridor to the mailboxes.

"Have you seen Josh yet?" Annie asked. "You'll have to thank him for the cards and the flowers."

Jennifer batted her on the arm. "Ha ha, very funny. I bet if he had a crush on you, you wouldn't think it was so funny."

"Hey, speaking of crushes, there's one you should know about. A girl in Nicole's cabin, Marian or Mary or something like that, has a major crush on Andy," Annie said.

"Andy Brenner?"

Annie nodded. "She made him a special painted pillowcase in arts and crafts the other day, with his name on it. When I asked him about it later, he turned all red. Gil told me that she's left other stuff at his cabin for him, too."

Jennifer giggled. "Poor Andy. Can you imagine if a thirteen-year-old boy had a crush on you?"

"I don't want to think about it." Annie grimaced. "But anyway, what are you going to do about Josh?"

"Ignore him, I guess," Jennifer said. "Maybe he'll get the hint."

"That's not very nice," Annie said. "Why not just tell him how you feel? Oh, I forgot—you don't like the direct approach. Why don't you write him a letter and tell him you're not interested? Kind of the reverse of the Brett plan."

"You know, if you keep teasing me so much, I might just go back to the infirmary," Jennifer complained. She opened her mailbox and pulled out an envelope with her parents' return address on it, in very sloppy handwriting. "Looks as if this is from one of my brothers."

Annie pulled on Jennifer's sleeve. "Did you hear that?"

"What?"

"That." Annie pointed down the hall toward the pay phone.

"But, Mother, I'm miserable here! How many times do I have to tell you that? You can't tell me just to stick it out, that it'll get better. It's *not* getting better."

"Sounds as though Nicole's as thrilled with camp as ever," Jennifer said. "Boy, I haven't missed hearing her complain all the time."

"*Shh,*" Annie said. "She'll hear you."

"Mother, you're the one who stuck me here in the first place!" Nicole said. "And if you won't come get me, at least give me your calling-card number so I can call Daddy."

"Jen, come on," Annie whispered. "We shouldn't listen in."

"Why not? This is good," Jennifer said.

Annie pulled on her arm until it was too painful to keep resisting, and Jennifer reluctantly followed her back into the dining room, which was filling up quickly for lunch.

"Do you think Nicole's serious about wanting to leave?" Annie asked.

"I don't see why she'd want to, after she snagged my job," Jennifer said.

"What do you mean?" Annie asked as they made their way over to the JCs' table. Lunch was the only meal that they ate together as a group—the rest of the time they were with their cabins.

"While I was sick, she got my lifeguarding job, and Mara says she gets to keep it, at least for this week," Jennifer said. "She said she wants to give Nicole the chance to try another activity, since she hates the meadow so much."

"Really? That's unusual," Annie said. "But you can't really blame Nicole—it was Mara's decision."

*Oh, yes I can,* Jennifer thought. She knew Nicole was only interested in working down at the waterfront because it had been her job. And she was sure that Nicole loved sticking her with meadow activities—not that Jennifer wouldn't have fun with them. She liked any outdoor activity, just as the campers seemed to. It was just that it was Nicole's job, not hers. She wondered what Andy was going to think when Nicole showed up at the waterfront that afternoon for the first time. Would he remember what a jerk she'd been to him—or fall in love all over again?

"Guess what?" Zoe greeted Nicole at the front door of Girls' Thirteen after lunch, looking excited. "Dee lost five pounds while she was in the infirmary. We're going to give her some of the left-over cookies from last night so she can gain some weight back."

Dee groaned. "Just what I need!"

Nicole smiled at Dee. "Glad to be back?" Dee had just returned from the infirmary—Nicole had spent her final night and morning being solely responsible for the cabin. Unfortunately, it had stopped raining, so they hadn't gone to Woodstock. But at least they'd been able to spend time outside, going for a short horseback ride, and then taking a walk through the woods. Nicole was relieved to have Dee back, but at the same time she felt a twinge of regret, as if she were being left out of something now.

Dee did look a little thinner than usual, but there was a healthy glow on her cheeks. "Thanks for holding down the fort while I was sick. I hear you did a great job."

"Oh, I don't know about that," Nicole said. She felt embarrassed, as if Dee were paying her a compliment for something she really didn't deserve. She hadn't done much, anyway.

"Katy and everyone were just filling me in on everything that happened while I was away," Dee said. "Have the girls written their parents yet this week?"

"Whoops." Katy hit her forehead with her hand. "We forgot about that."

"I usually ask them to write home every Monday, at least," Dee said. "Some of them are pretty good about writing to their parents, but others wouldn't do it all summer if we didn't make them. No wonder they didn't remind you. Since it's rest hour, we might as well get started now."

Nicole usually spent rest hour hanging out with the other JCs in the counselors' lounge, but since she hadn't been able to during the past few days, she was out of the routine. She didn't feel like rushing back there, either. What fun was it sitting around watching Gil and Annie cuddle and having Eliot and Jennifer criticize her? She might as well just hang out with her cabin for a little while longer.

"I just *wrote* to them," Marian complained.

"We thought we didn't have to write this week, since you were sick," Zoe said.

"Come on, get out your pens and paper, everybody. You can't do anything else until I see a completed letter," Dee said firmly.

"Can't we at least go outside to do it?" Lynne asked. "We've been trapped in here for three straight days."

"Not until you're finished," said Dee.

"I wish *you* were still our counselor," Casey whispered to Nicole as she walked past on the way to her bunk bed.

Mimi, meanwhile, had already gotten out a notebook and was starting to write. She was lying quietly on her bed.

"Why don't we just get Mimi to write our letters for us," Zoe said. "She's so *good* at writing letters home."

"Cut it out," Mimi said, looking up with hurt eyes.

"Yeah," Nicole said without thinking. "Write your own letter, Zoe, the way Dee told you to, and stop procrastinating."

Mimi looked surprised by this sudden show of support from Nicole—as surprised as Zoe looked to hear Nicole defend her.

Dee smiled approvingly at Nicole. "You heard her, Zoe. Get started, now. I'll be coming around to see how you're doing in a few minutes."

Mimi went back to her letter, and Zoe pulled

herself up onto her top bunk and got some stationery from the shelf beside her bed.

"Dee, I think I'll go take a walk, if that's okay with you," Nicole said. Suddenly she felt as if she needed some time by herself.

"Sure." Dee patted her on the arm. "And thanks again for being such a good replacement for me. You should be proud of yourself. I know it wasn't easy, especially with the weather."

Nicole shrugged, feeling tongue-tied. She wasn't used to being praised, and she didn't know what to say in reply. Fortunately, Dee turned to help Betsy refill her cartridge pen, and Nicole slipped out the door and headed for the lake.

The minute she was alone, her mother's words started to echo in her head. "I can't possibly come now, sweetheart. If you knew how busy I've been . . . and I have friends here. I can't just up and leave. I'm sorry you don't like it there, but you're going to have to stick it out."

Nicole couldn't remember ever asking her mother for something this important before. And what was her response? What mattered most to her right now? Her new "friend," whatever his name was. She probably hadn't even gone to Arizona for back treatments in the first place—there'd been a man involved all along. Nicole was sure of it.

Nicole wandered in the direction of the lake, her eyes filling with tears. She couldn't remember ever feeling so isolated. She still hadn't reached her father, but it didn't really matter. She knew what he would say. Something like, "You've started this, and you're going to finish it." He thought quitting was the easy way out of things, and he said so often enough that Nicole knew his routine by heart. It didn't matter if she was unhappy—what mattered was that she do the job right.

She'd thought she could depend on her mother. She'd pictured how her mother would come to her rescue, driving up in front of the Lodge in a glamorous sports car. She'd probably have a ton of southwestern jewelry for Nicole, and she'd laugh her head off when she saw the Shack. "Let's get you *out* of here," she'd say, and within the hour they would have packed up Nicole's things and been headed for a *real* lodge in the mountains, or down to the city for an elegant dinner at one of their favorite restaurants.

But now, instead of rescuing Nicole, all her mother wanted to do was spend time with her new boyfriend. Obviously she cared more about him than she did about Nicole, her only child.

Nicole took a deep breath and crouched down on the beach, tracing her name in the sand with a stick. She was still determined to stick to her plan—if anything, the conversation with her mother that noon had made her more determined. If her mother didn't want her, and her father was out of touch, it wasn't going to stop her from leaving Kissamee. Let them try to find her when she was gone—then they'd realize she'd meant it when she said she was miserable. It would serve them right.

She was so absorbed in her thoughts that she jumped when she heard someone call her name. It was Eliot, coming down the path around the lake. "Out on parole?" he asked, coming closer. "Did they finally release you from Girls' Thirteen?"

Nicole kept writing in the sand. "Yeah, Dee's back from the infirmary. Why aren't you at the lounge with everyone else?"

"I could ask the same of you," Eliot replied.

Nicole sighed. Why did Eliot have to make everything so difficult? Couldn't he just leave her alone?

"Actually, I just wanted to spend some time outside, after all that rain—well, you know," Eliot said. "Anyway, Tim wants me to go into Middlebrook and pick up some stuff for him before afternoon activities start. Want to come along?"

*That's right,* Nicole remembered. *Eliot has a car!* "Where are you going?" she asked.

"The post office, to get a bunch of stamps to sell at the Lodge, and the supermarket for some kitchen supplies," Eliot said.

Nicole didn't have to think about it long. Even if Eliot wasn't always easy to be with, it did mean a ride in a car—on an open road. And if she got to know Eliot better, maybe she could convince him to let her borrow his car. Besides, Eliot looked even cuter today than he usually did. His eyes were such a great shade of blue, she thought, standing up beside him. "I'd love to," she said, brushing sand off her hands.

"It's kind of weird," Eliot said as they walked back toward the parking lot where he kept his car. "I keep thinking that we must have met each other before camp. You never go to any of the parties at Tyler, do you?"

Nicole shook her head. She was about to make a comment about how she wouldn't be caught dead at a high-school party—or with a high-school boy—but she caught herself. Eliot was being nice. Maybe it wouldn't hurt to try being nice to him, too.

"Do your parents belong to the yacht club? Maybe we bumped into each other there," Eliot said as they climbed into the car.

"No. My father likes boats, but he lives in Connecticut," Nicole explained. "He and my mother are divorced."

Eliot nodded. "So we didn't meet there. . . . Where else could it have been?"

Nicole shrugged, rolling down her window as they pulled out of the long road that led up to the camp grounds. The breeze blowing through her hair felt wonderful, and she didn't care if it ended up looking messy. Whom was she going to run into, anyway? "Did you have a nice visit with your dad on Dead Day?"

"Yeah. It was all right," Eliot said. "But he must have asked me a hundred times what I was going to do with my life *after* camp. You can't be a counselor forever, you know.' " He imitated his father's deep voice.

Nicole laughed. "Does he seriously think you'd want to be?"

"I know! I mean, I told him, I'm going to college in a year, and then I'll figure out what to do with my life. Not *now.*" Eliot shook his head, making a left turn onto the town's main street.

"Yeah, my dad can be like that, too. He's into big plans. But . . . I guess I wish I saw him as often as you see yours. He travels a lot on business, and when he is home, I don't see him, either, because I live with my mother," Nicole explained.

"Well, to tell you the truth, I don't see my dad all that often, either," Eliot said. "What's your mother like?"

"She's too wrapped up in her love life to worry about me," Nicole blurted out. "She wouldn't notice if I ended up selling hot dogs at Shea Stadium for a living."

Eliot laughed. "Come on, I bet she's not that bad."

Nicole glared at him, but she could feel her lower lip trembling. *Don't cry,* she told herself. *Just don't.* "She is," Nicole said. "She's completely ruined my entire summer just so she could go to Arizona, supposedly to get her back fixed. Only now that she's in love with someone, she probably won't even come back at the end of the summer. We'll have to move to Arizona. Then they'll break up, and I'll be stuck in some dumb high school all the way out in Arizona—"

"Just the way you were stuck here?" Eliot interrupted.

"Exactly," Nicole said. She looked at Eliot, who was smiling at her. "What's so funny?"

"You are! I mean, you think that this whole summer has absolutely *nothing* to do with you," Eliot said.

"If I had my way, it *wouldn't* have anything to do with me," Nicole replied. She thought about the time she'd spent with Girls' Thirteen. So far, that was the *only* thing she wouldn't want to forget completely once she left.

"But if you don't try to make it into something you like, you'll never have a good time." Eliot pulled into a parking space just outside the post office.

"Exactly. And in order for me to like this camp, it would have to be completely different," Nicole said.

Eliot shut off the motor. "What would you change?"

Nicole tapped her fingers against the door. "For one thing, I'd make sure it was close to civilization."

"Okay, but then you might not have Torch Lake. And you have to admit, it's a very nice lake," Eliot said.

"I'd change some of the rules, so that we had more days off," Nicole continued, ignoring him. "And I'd change the Shack, so that it was big enough for six people. No, scratch that—I'd get rid of some of the people."

"Like who?" Eliot prompted, smiling.

Nicole was becoming fed up with the whole conversation. Why did she feel as if Eliot were digging for information? "What about you? Don't tell me you love everything about Kissamee."

Eliot shrugged. "I think it works pretty well, all things considered. This is the ninth summer I've been here, you know."

"Are you insane?" Nicole stared at him. "You came *back*?"

"Nicole! Come on, you're the one who's crazy. By the time you finally decide to like this place, it'll be the last day of camp."

"No, I think I'll split before that happens," Nicole retorted. "Look, just get the dumb stamps. I don't want to be late—it's my first day down on the waterfront."

"So you *do* like working here," Eliot said, shutting the door. "If you didn't, you wouldn't care if you were on time." He winked at her, then ran up the post-office steps.

*What* is *it with him?* Nicole wondered. He seemed to enjoy giving her a hard time. For some reason, Eliot had decided that it was up to him to convince Nicole to like camp. What business was it of his, anyway? Just because they were from the same city didn't mean they saw everything the same way—obviously. He sounded just like her mother.

Everyone wanted her to give camp another chance. Nicole had given Camp Kissamee about as many chances as it deserved. What about someone giving *her* a break, for once?

# CHAPTER
## NINE

"Nicole, it's so nice to have you back," Lisa said on Thursday morning, as everyone got dressed before flagpole. "I was beginning to feel sort of lonely in the back room all by myself."

"Lonely? In here?" Nicole replied. "That'll be the day." She had only been back at the Shack for one night, and already she felt sick of it.

"The Comps really start today!" Megan said in an excited voice. "Can you believe it?"

"I know, after those three days of torrential rain, I thought it was going to have to be all water events. But it looks as if the ground pretty much dried out yesterday," Beth added.

*Thrillsville.* Nicole rolled her eyes as she looked at her reflection in one of the bathroom mirrors. She didn't even know why she was bothering to brush her hair. From the sound of some of the events, she was going to be facedown in the mud soon enough. If there were any way to get out of the Comps, she hadn't thought of it.

"Hey, Nicole, how's everything down at the waterfront?" Jennifer yelled from the front section of the cabin.

Nicole gritted her teeth. "Just fine!" she called back, in a phony, cheerful voice. "How's archery going?"

"I like it," Jennifer answered, coming over to stand outside the bathroom door. "Guess how many bull's-eyes I got yesterday?"

"I couldn't possibly," Nicole said. "One?"

"No, thirteen," Jennifer said with a smile. "Andy told me you had your hands full yesterday, with all the swimmers wanting lessons and practicing for the Comps races. He said you hardly had time to breathe."

Nicole shrugged. It had been busy—at times she had wanted to swim away and go sit on the float way out in the middle of the lake. But she'd stuck with it, even though Andy had been less than helpful, in her opinion. It seemed as if every camper had wanted to swim after having been cooped up inside during the storm. It wasn't as if she couldn't handle it, though. "We took care of everyone just fine," Nicole told Jennifer. "Actually, I'm really looking forward to it this afternoon."

"It figures," Jennifer grumbled, walking away.

Nicole felt a small sense of satisfaction. Maybe now Jennifer would know what it was like for someone to try to make her life miserable. Maybe she'd stop giving Nicole such a hard time about every-thing.

*And maybe cows will fly*, Nicole thought.

"Nicole, how come you're not wearing any gray?" Zoe asked when Nicole sat down with the girls in her cabin at flagpole on Thursday morning.

"Look at how much blue we have on," Marian said. She, Zoe, and Janet were decked out from head to toe in various shades of blue. Some of the shades didn't exactly go together, but the overall effect was impressive. The other girls had at least one item of clothing with their color on it. Glancing around at all the campers, Nicole saw a sea of blue and gray.

"You guys look great," she said. "Very blue."

Dee and Katy had both gotten into the spirit for Comps, too. Dee was on the blue team, and she had woven blue ribbons into her curly hair. Katy looked even paler than usual in a gray T-shirt and white shorts. "I figure they'll be gray by the time the day's over, anyway," she said when she saw Nicole looking at her. "Isn't this fun? Everyone's so excited!"

"Yeah, I guess," Nicole said. Personally, there were several other things she'd rather be doing—such as sleeping.

"I think it's so important," Katy continued. "This kind of competition really helps the kids let off steam, in a positive way. Believe me, our girls are ready for it."

Nicole groaned softly. Only Katy could see the

Comps as some sort of therapy. Even though it wasn't particularly Nicole's kind of thing, she could tell it was simply supposed to be *fun*.

Brett, wearing a blue shirt and gray shorts, blew on his whistle a few times to get everyone's attention. "Is everybody ready?" he shouted, once they were all quiet.

"Ready to win!" one boy wearing blue cried.

"Not!" a girl dressed in gray answered.

The whole crowd started to cheer in support of the two teams. It took Brett a minute to get everyone quiet again. "Now, let me just tell you how things are going to work today. The object is to score as many points for your team as possible between now and Saturday night. Since we're starting so late, we'll be canceling all other activities and just doing Comps for the next three days. Today we'll have the soccer game, archery competition, horseshoes, wheelbarrow race—and those are just for starters. We have six other races lined up for today, which we'll announce at lunchtime. So, I hope you're ready to put forward your best effort for your team!"

"But remember!" Mara said, jumping up to stand beside Brett, "safety comes first."

"Does she have to ruin everything?" Zoe complained.

Nicole tried not to smile, but she couldn't help it.

"This is just a game. If you don't win, it's not the end of the world," Mara droned on. "And I don't want to hear about any dirty tricks, like the one we had last year when someone ripped out the strings of the opposing team's badminton rackets and they couldn't hit a thing."

"Sounds pretty fun to me," Janet said.

Dee gave her a stern look. "You can win without being sneaky, you know."

"We'll tell everyone the day's total score at dinner tonight!" Brett called. "You'd better all eat a big breakfast—you're going to need all your strength!"

With that, the campers gave one final cheer and jumped up to run into the Lodge. Nicole didn't see the need to hurry for Wally's food. Everyone in the cabin took off without her, except Mimi.

"I wish I were on the blue team," Mimi said shyly. "Marian, Zoe, and Janet are all blue. They look as though they're having so much fun. Gray isn't even a color—not a *real* color."

Nicole was trying to think of something reassuring to say when Eliot passed her on his way into the Lodge, following the boys in his cabin. "Hi," he said, a little stiffly. They hadn't spoken since their trip into Middlebrook, which hadn't exactly ended on a good note.

"Hi," Nicole said, not meeting his eyes.

"You're not wearing a color," he said. Eliot was wearing a blue bandanna, which he'd tied around his neck.

"I don't feel like wearing any gray. It looks awful on me," Nicole admitted. "Besides, I think this whole thing is stupid."

"You're kidding," Eliot said. "And I thought you'd be beside yourself with excitement."

"What's that supposed to mean?" Nicole asked.

"Well, good luck! May the best New Yorker win!" Eliot jumped up the steps two at a time and vanished into the Lodge.

Nicole had a snappy retort on the tip of her tongue, but she bit it back.

"He's cute, don't you think?" asked Mimi.

Nicole frowned. "Don't tell me *you* have a crush on a counselor, too," she said.

Mimi giggled. "No! I don't," she said. "I just think that if I were you, I'd think he's pretty cute. He's nice, too. He helped me practice at horseshoes yesterday."

"Yeah, he's nice," Nicole said. Maybe to Mimi he was, anyway. He *was* cute, too. But Eliot seemed to think it was his job to needle Nicole, and she couldn't understand why. He kept wanting her to be happier at camp. What did it matter to him?

"First one to drink her orange juice gets ten points," Zoe said just as Nicole and Mimi reached their table in the dining room. All the girls at the table gulped down their glasses of juice, then screamed, "Finished!"

"If you guys race to finish your breakfast, you're going to be sorry," Dee warned them.

"I know—let's see who can eat the *most* pancakes," Janet said.

"Don't forget, you're going to be running around in a few hours," Dee said.

"We could have a competition to see who lives after eating this fruit salad," Nicole said, and everyone started laughing.

"That reminds me," Lynne said. "What about the points we were supposed to get for cleaning the cabin?"

Nicole looked at Katy. "Uh, well—those are bonus points," she said.

"What do you mean?" asked Janet.

"Yeah, we worked hard for that," said Casey.

"Don't worry, they'll count," Katy said. "Brett knows the blue team won."

"Yeah, but he didn't say anything about a cabin-cleaning competition," Janet complained.

"You tricked us," Lynne said. "No fair."

"You passed inspection, didn't you?" Nicole asked. "If you hadn't, you'd probably be cleaning out the stables right now."

Casey frowned. "Yeah, I guess."

Dee grinned at Nicole. "Good idea," she mouthed.

"It was Katy's," Nicole whispered back.

"Well, the blue team's going to win, anyway, even without those points," Zoe declared. "Hey, Marian, what team is Andy on?"

"Gray," Marian said, her eyes fixed on Andy's back. He was sitting across the dining room. "I knew they'd separate us by putting us on different teams."

Katy turned to Dee and Nicole and shook her head. "She's still infatuated with him."

"I remember my first big crush," Dee said to Nicole. "I thought I was going to die when he started dating another girl. Now it seems so trivial when I compare it to other problems I've had since then."

Nicole nodded. "I know what you mean." She'd give anything to be suffering from a silly crush—and not a major case of unhappiness. If only the solution were easier. She'd made up her mind to leave on Saturday—only two days from now. She could hardly wait.

"Come on!" Jennifer screamed at the top of her lungs.

"Careful, you'll lose your voice," Andy warned, coming up beside her.

"No, I won't," Jennifer said. "Come on, Cheryl! She's in my cabin," she told Andy. They were at the wheelbarrow races watching different groups of three compete for their team. Cathy was recording the results, with Danny Gluck, the head counselor of Boys' Eight, helping. "So far six blue teams have won, and only *two* gray have won." She pointed at Andy's gray T-shirt. "We're going to bury you."

"You probably will," Andy agreed, surveying the field.

"What? Is this the same I'll-win-or-else Brenner I used to know? The one who's been trying for the past five years to get me back for hitting a home run off his pitch when we were twelve?" Jennifer asked.

"Okay, I still want to win, *but*. You'll see why I said that when I tell you that I have been paired with a certain person for the wheelbarrow race," Andy said. "I'll give you a hint. This person is not wearing one speck of gray. She says it's not one of her colors."

"No way! You and Nicole—on a team?" Jennifer said. "Well, I shouldn't be surprised. Now that you work on the waterfront together, you're probably becoming best friends."

Andy raised one eyebrow. "Right. Jen, promise me you'll come back next week. Do whatever you have to do. Plead, beg, bribe—"

"It's that bad?" asked Jennifer. "I thought you'd decided to ask Nicole out again."

"I was only joking when I said that," Andy said. "You thought I was serious? Please! Give me a little more credit."

"I'll try to come back, but I don't know if they'll let me," Jennifer said. "Mara said she wanted to give Nicole a chance to do something else here this summer."

"So let her teach beauty classes," Andy said. "I mean, she's not bad on the water. She's a good swimmer, and she knows what she's doing and everything. I just don't have anything to say to her. And I feel like an idiot, knowing that she knows how much I liked her!"

"I heard her talking to her mother the other day. She asked her to come pick her up," Jennifer said, just as there was a loud cheer from the winning team. "All right, blues!" she screamed. "Anyway, if she leaves, then none of us will have to worry about dealing with her anymore."

"Do you really think she'd leave? What would be the point?" Andy asked. "She's made it this far."

Jennifer shrugged. "She probably has some back-to-school shopping to do. Beats me." Actually, she had been thinking a lot about the conversation between Nicole and her mother that she and Annie had overheard. Deep down, Jennifer had never given much thought to Nicole's being truly unhappy. She'd thought that Nicole was simply a grump, used to manipulating people to get what she wanted. That was the first time she'd heard Nicole ask for something so directly. Jennifer couldn't understand why anyone would want to leave Kissamee—she'd been coming for years, and she loved it. But it felt like home to her—and she could see that it didn't feel that way to Nicole. Still, what was she supposed to do? If Nicole didn't make any effort and walked around putting down camp all the time, how was she going to see how much it had to offer?

"Jennifer, I saw your race. You were terrific."

Jennifer had been lost in her thoughts and hadn't even seen Josh walk up to her. He was wearing a blue-and-gray striped T-shirt. When he saw her looking at it, he shrugged. "What can I say, it was the only gray I had."

Jennifer smiled. Josh was funny, good-looking, and incredibly nice. So why didn't she like him? She didn't feel any of the fireworks you were supposed to feel when you fell in love. She wanted to be just friends with him.

"All right, blue!" she yelled, cheering on the next team. She felt awkward around Josh, who now seemed to hang on her every word whenever they spoke.

"The hayride's only a couple of days away," Josh said, looking eagerly into her eyes.

She focused on the field, where Andy and Nicole were about to race. "Yeah, well, it might rain," she said.

"Really?" Josh sounded crestfallen.

"Blue, beat gray! Blue, beat gray!" Jennifer started a chant on the sidelines as Andy and Nicole lined up at the starting line. Megan was the other member of the team. During Comps, the younger cabins raced against one another, and the older cabins did the same, to keep things fair. Darcy, Eliot, and Michael were on the blue team.

"Don't tell me you want me to get down on the ground," Jennifer heard Nicole complain.

"Both hands," Andy said. "Megan will take one foot and I'll take the other. All you have to do is keep moving one hand in front of the other as fast as you can."

"Why can't I do the steering?" Nicole said. Andy glanced over toward Jennifer and winked.

"Wheelbarrows, take your positions!" Cathy instructed. Nicole seemed to give in, dropping down on all fours. Cathy blew the starting whistle, and the campers on the sidelines started to shriek their support.

"Quit pushing so hard!" Nicole yelled on her way down the field.

"Faster, Nicole, faster!" some of the girls in her cabin screamed.

"Go, Darcy!" Jennifer yelled, trying not to laugh. The sight of Nicole flying across the field on her hands, her usually neat hair swinging in her face, was too much for Jennifer. She collapsed on the ground, shrieking hysterically. She'd bet Nicole had never done anything like this in her life—and she was actually pretty good at it!

But Darcy's team pulled ahead at the last second, reaching the finish line first. Nicole collapsed on the ground as Andy and Megan let go of her legs. Jennifer stood up and walked over to congratulate Darcy.

Eliot reached out a hand to help Nicole to her feet, and she pushed it away, standing up on her own.

"Nice try," Megan said. "You did a great job!"

"Yeah, not bad for your first time," Eliot said, smiling.

"And last time," Nicole muttered, her face pink.

"Who ever heard of making seventeen-year-olds do wheelbarrow races?"

"Just wait for the egg-in-the-spoon race," Jennifer told her. "We all get to look like idiots in that one."

Nicole glowered at her. No, Jennifer decided, Nicole wasn't unhappy at camp. She was just *always* this grouchy.

"Jen, wait up! What's your next event?" Josh called, running after her.

Jennifer sighed. How was she going to tell Josh to leave her alone—nicely?

# CHAPTER
## TEN

The Lodge was practically empty. Nicole fished around in her pocket for the slip of paper with her mother's calling-card number on it. She'd finally convinced her to give it to her the other night so that she could leave a message for her father. She used to have her own card, until she ran up a couple of hundred dollars on it calling a boarding-school friend in Italy. Since then, she hadn't been able to call anyone.

Everyone was outside taking a "bug-juice break," as Jennifer called it. It was the middle of the afternoon, and they'd brought out huge containers of fruit punch as a break between the all-camp soccer game and all-camp baseball game. Nicole felt as if she were in training for the Olympic decathlon.

When she had punched in all the required numbers, Nicole heard the unmistakable pickup of her father's answering machine. "I'm not available to take your call at this time. If you wait for the beep . . ."

Nicole waited, then spoke. "Daddy, it's me. I'm

calling because there's a problem I need to talk to you about. If you could call me back as soon as possible, just leave a message with the head of camp and—"

"Nicole?" Her father's voice came on the line. Nicole wanted to jump up and down, she was so happy.

"Daddy! It's so great to hear your voice. I thought I'd never reach you! What are you doing home in the middle of the afternoon?"

"I'm in from France for a few days, and I have a big deal I'm trying to finish some paperwork on. It has to be faxed to Tokyo tomorrow morning. There were too many distractions at the office, so I came home, and I'm screening my calls," her father said.

*He didn't even ask how I am,* Nicole thought. He made it sound as if she were just another bothersome interruption.

"But I'm never too busy to talk to you," he added. "Now, did you say there's a problem?"

*Typical Daddy—he gets right to the heart of the matter,* Nicole thought. No small talk. "Yeah, there is a problem. Daddy, I know you said this camp was supposed to be a great learning experience for me, but it isn't working out."

"Really? Why's that?" Her father sounded distant and bored.

Nicole bit her lip. Why did she get the feeling that he was still doing paperwork, even while he was talking to her?

"There're a few things. The other girls in my cabin are awful. They've done so many things to try to bug me, playing practical jokes, and—"

"Now, Nicole," Mr. Talbot interrupted, "just because you've had some sort of tiff with a few of your cabinmates is no reason to get hysterical."

"It isn't just a *tiff*, Daddy." Nicole's eyes filled with tears. "Believe me, it's much worse than that. Mother keeps telling me to give it a chance. Well, I have. You always say that you can't judge something until you've really tried it. I've tried it and I hate it! I want to come home," she said desperately. A tear trickled down her cheek.

"You know your mother and I think Kissamee is the best place for you to be this summer," her father said. He sounded so calm and reasonable that Nicole wanted to shriek.

"I know that's what you said. But if you knew how miserable I am—"

"And, anyway," her father cut in, "I'm afraid it's impossible for you to come home. I'm headed off to France again at the end of this week. After that, there's a conference on the West Coast. That reminds me—how's your mother?"

Nicole thought of her mother's new "friend." "Fine," she said. "She can't come back from Arizona until the end of August, though."

"You see? It's the best thing for you just to stay put right now." Her father sounded as if he'd taken care of a big problem and was pleased with himself

117

for getting it—in this case, her—out of his way. "Nicole, you know how I feel about quitters. You have a job to do there, your very first job. I'd like to see you stick it out, however hard it is."

Nicole didn't know what else to say. She was about to start crying in earnest, and she knew she had to get off the phone before she broke down completely. How could he be so unfeeling?

"I used to get homesick at camp, too." Mr. Talbot chuckled. "Pretty hard to believe, but your old man once begged his parents to let him come home, too. It was the first night of camp, and I was so lonely. My father told me to see how things looked in the morning. By that time I was friends with everyone in the cabin, and when they came to pick me up at the end of the summer, I didn't want to leave!"

Nicole felt her chest constrict with pain. "Daddy, this isn't my first night. I've been here five weeks," she reminded him.

"Believe me, Nicole, this is going to turn out to be one of the best summers of your life," her father went on, cheerfully ignoring her comment. "Now, I'd better get back to this project, or I won't be able to foot the bill for that school of yours next fall!"

Nicole made circles on her dirt-covered legs with her finger. Was that all he was going to say? Didn't he care that she was so unhappy?

"I'll bring you back something from my trip," he said. "It'll be waiting for you the next time you visit.

Now, be a good girl. We'll talk again soon. Have a swim in Torch Lake for me, will you?"

And that was it. He was gone. Nicole leaned her head against the cold metal of the phone, her heart pounding. She wondered what would happen if she called him back and screamed that she couldn't stand it anymore, that she would rather run away than "stick it out." Would he let the answering machine take her call?

Nicole heard a door slam, and she hurried to brush the tears off her face.

"Nicole, are you in here?" Eliot's voice called down the narrow corridor.

She didn't answer right away. Feeling as bad as she did, she couldn't face anybody. Eliot didn't give up, though. She heard his sneakers squeaking on the wooden floor, and a moment later he appeared beside her. "I thought I saw you come down here. Are you all done? Your team needs you to play outfield in the baseball game, and we can't continue the game without you."

"I'm lousy at baseball," Nicole said, her voice shaky.

"Hey, are you okay?" Eliot looked into her eyes. "Have you been crying?"

Nicole shrugged. "I'm just upset with my parents, that's all."

"Yeah?" Eliot looked genuinely sympathetic, and Nicole decided to confide in him—a little. Maybe it would help to talk to someone about what was going on.

"They just . . . don't have any time for me." Nicole pulled her hair back from her face. "That's why they dumped me here this summer, and that's partly why I hate it so much. Now that I'm unhappy, they won't come to get me, either."

"You're serious? You want to leave?" Eliot asked.

"More than anything," Nicole said. "In fact, I—" She stopped. She wasn't going to tell anyone that she was going to leave, no matter what. Not even a torrential rainstorm, or a hurricane, could keep her from sticking to her plan.

"You what?" asked Eliot.

"Nothing," Nicole said. "Anyway, it doesn't matter because they won't come get me. So it looks as if I'm stuck."

"Good," Eliot said.

"Thanks a lot!" Nicole started to walk down the hall.

Eliot followed her. "All I meant was, I'm glad you're sticking around. Remember I told you I don't see my dad much, either? He's always incredibly busy and doesn't seem to have time for me. But even if I don't see him all the time, I know he still cares about me."

Nicole glanced over at Eliot. They did seem to have a lot in common, after all. She felt as if he understood her—he knew what it was like to have parents who seemed too busy to care.

"Anyway, you wouldn't want to miss the hayride on Sunday night," Eliot teased her. "I know that for a fact."

Nicole smiled, despite herself. "Not a lot of people know this, but I am seriously allergic to hay."

"Is that so?" Eliot pushed open the screen door, and they walked out onto the large wraparound porch. "So you're really looking forward to this, huh?"

"Oh, definitely," Nicole said. "Hayrides rank right up there with baseball and archery."

"Don't forget flagpole," Eliot said. "I know it's one of your personal favorites." They walked over toward the baseball field in silence for a few minutes. "You know, I was just thinking—since I've got my car here and everything, and I know you've been feeling kind of down lately, how would you like to go to Ryan's tomorrow for lunch? It'd be a good break from you-know-who's cooking."

Nicole looked at Eliot. He was wearing khaki shorts and a blue polo shirt that made his eyes seem even bluer than usual. He really did look great. "I don't know, Eliot," she said, suddenly feeling shy. "I have a lot on my mind."

"We could talk, if you want," Eliot said. "Or we could just sit there and drink milk shakes."

"Are you sure we can leave in the middle of the afternoon, just like that?" asked Nicole. "I got in trouble with Mara for skipping lunch once. And there's no way I'm going to mop that kitchen floor again."

"She made you mop the kitchen floor? Harsh," Eliot said. "Well, we eat lunch together as JCs, right? Nothing says we can't eat together in another location."

"Mara will come up with a reason," Nicole said. "Trust me."

"Okay. I'll ask Brett about it. Maybe we can say we're going to town to do an errand but have lunch instead," Eliot suggested.

"Don't tell me that Eliot Packard is going against the precious camp rules," Nicole teased him.

"For a good reason, of course I will." Eliot looked slightly embarrassed. "Actually, I've been wanting to ask you out for a while. But you're pretty intimidating, you know that? Every time I got close enough to talk to you, you acted as if you'd rather be boiled in oil than associate with me."

"Me? What about you?" Nicole said. "You didn't even talk to me the first two weeks of camp."

"I didn't talk to you? You didn't talk to me," Eliot said.

Nicole raised one eyebrow. "What's the difference?"

"There's a big difference. Anyway, do you want to go or not?" Eliot asked as they reached the baseball diamond at the edge of the meadow.

"Sure," Nicole said, feeling a little shy, "I'd like to." It was strange—she hadn't been on a "date" since she got to camp. She wondered if Eliot meant it that way.

"Nicole, grab a glove and get in left field!" Tim called to her from the small set of bleachers.

"I always thought you belonged there," Eliot said as she jogged off toward home plate.

Was Eliot truly interested? And if he was, was she? Usually Nicole went after guys she couldn't have: her French teacher, a guy who worked in her father's office, and then Gil. She'd never thought about dating someone like Eliot, who came from the same kind of world she did.

*It's only lunch at a dive with a jukebox,* she reminded herself as she ran out to left field. Still, she was excited about it. Maybe sticking it out hadn't been such a bad idea, after all.

"Are you thinking of leaving or something?" Jennifer said, standing in the doorway between the Shack's two rooms and staring at the clothes piled on Nicole's bed.

"What makes you say that?" Nicole replied, looking startled.

"It just looks as though you're packing, that's all." Jennifer tucked a loose strand of hair into her ponytail. "I thought you might have given up."

Nicole frowned. "Why, because my team is behind in some stupid game?"

"Behind is putting it mildly," Jennifer said. "If

you guys don't watch out, you're going to get skunked."

"'Skunked'? What's that?" asked Nicole. "Oh, I know. I suppose it's one of Camp Kissamee's traditions to have the losers sprayed by a skunk."

Megan entered the back room and laughed. "That *would* be pretty funny, but that's not it. Skunked means you don't get to a hundred points before the other team wins. But, Jennifer, that's not going to happen—is it, Nicole?"

Nicole didn't answer. She was still trying to figure out if Jennifer knew something.

"So what are all the clothes for?" Jennifer asked again.

"Don't be so nosey!" Annie called from the other room.

"Really, Jen," Beth said. "You're acting like a detective or something."

"It just seems kind of strange, that's all," Jennifer said.

Nicole wasn't about to tell her that she was trying to pick out something to wear on her unofficial date with Eliot. She could hear Jennifer teasing her even now, saying things like: "Do you think Eliot would actually be interested in someone like you? He's too down-to-earth."

"Actually . . ." Jennifer sat down on Lisa's bed. Lisa was on a late-night walk with Michael before lights-out. "I overheard you saying something, and I wanted to know if it was true." She seemed nervous for some reason.

"Yes, it's true—I hate wheelbarrow races," Nicole said, hoping that would convince Jennifer to leave her alone. She was getting a little sick of bickering with Jennifer. It took too much effort, and there wasn't much point to it. The truth was, Nicole couldn't quite remember what had bugged her so much about Jennifer or the others in the first place. Annie was another story—they'd gotten off on the wrong foot because of Gil. But she even felt less intensely jealous of Annie than she had a few days ago.

It wasn't like Nicole to admit, even to herself, that there were times lately when she found herself just wanting to relax, hang out with them, let down her guard. Sometimes, when she listened to Annie and Jennifer clowning around or Megan and Beth confiding in each other, she felt as if it would be great to be friends with them instead of their constant enemy. But it was too late to change that now.

"No," Jennifer said. "What I heard was you saying something about leaving. Is it true? Are you leaving camp?"

Nicole tried to read Jennifer's expression. Normally, she would expect Jennifer to be happy—no, ecstatic—at the thought of her leaving. But Jennifer looked truly concerned for once.

"What do you mean, leaving?" Beth asked. "You can't leave."

Nicole shrugged. "I've thought about it."

"No one's ever left in the middle of the summer," Megan said. "Not that I can remember, anyway. What about your cabin?"

"Yeah, what about Girls' Thirteen? They'd really miss you," Annie said, coming to stand in the doorway.

"I doubt it," Nicole mumbled.

"So what's the deal?" asked Jennifer. "Are you taking off?"

The way Jennifer got right to the point reminded Nicole of her father. "It's none of your business," she said.

"But you've thought about it," Jennifer pressed.

Nicole couldn't take the interrogation any longer. "Yes, of course I've thought about it!" she said. "I think about it every day. And the way things are going, I just might do it!"

"Nicole, how could you? You know how much Tim and Cathy are depending on you," Beth said.

"All I know is I can't stand it here," Nicole said. "So I asked my mother to come visit me this Sunday. We're going to go for a drive, and let's just say that I might come back, and I might not." As soon as the words were out of her mouth, Nicole wanted to take them back. It was one thing if she decided to leave on her own—she could manage that. But now she'd lied, and she'd have to find a way to pull it off, or else be humiliated.

Annie looked shocked. So did Megan and Beth.

Only Jennifer didn't seem very surprised. "You really want to get out of here that much?" she asked.

"Well, I was starting to think things were getting better, but I'm not sure," Nicole said, stuffing things back into the drawers beneath her bed.

"I'm sorry," Jennifer said. "I just wanted to know if it was true. I guess I shouldn't have butted in." She got up and walked back into the front bedroom, and the others followed her.

Nicole let her head rest against the wool blanket on top of her bed. For a second, Jennifer had almost sounded as if she was trying to apologize. Maybe she hadn't meant to pry. But now, all because of her, Nicole had to find her way out of a lie. It wasn't going to be easy, and there might only be one solution: to leave before her mother was supposed to get there.

# CHAPTER
## ELEVEN

"Nicole seemed pretty frazzled last night," Annie said, as she and Jennifer watched the blue and gray teams compete in a game of touch football Friday morning. "Do you think she's really going to leave this weekend?"

"I don't know," Jennifer replied. "In a way, I hope so. She hasn't exactly added a lot to camp life. But then I think she's just bluffing, saying that to get attention, the same way she does everything else. Only this time she might really mean it."

Annie shook her head. "I don't know why I'm saying this, but I have a feeling she's starting to change a little bit. She seems to be softening up— toward me, you, camp, everything."

"The day Nicole Talbot softens up," Jennifer said, "will be the day Mara decides to burn her rule book! Face it, Annie. You always see the best in people. Remember what a creep she was to you just a few weeks ago?"

"Of course I do," Annie said. "But . . . she hasn't even given me a hard time about anything lately. She avoids me and Gil like the plague. I think she's finally accepted that there's nothing she can do to break us up."

Jennifer watched as Justin dropped back to pass the football. He sent it in a perfectly spiraling arc down the field to one of the boys from Cabin Thirteen. Secretly, she had a feeling Annie was right. Nicole hadn't changed overnight, but there was something about her that *was* different. She didn't seem so harsh anymore. But it wasn't as if she'd started being nice to everybody, either. *Then again, I haven't exactly been friendly to her.*

"Annie, to tell you the truth, this whole situation with Nicole has really been bothering me," Jennifer admitted.

"Really?" Annie said. "How come?"

Jennifer wasn't sure herself. "I guess . . . I don't know. I'm not used to not being able to get along with someone—especially someone I live with. At first, Nicole was so ready to hate this place, and all of us, that I just wanted to give it right back to her. But lately, she's seemed more . . . *human* or something. I guess I just don't know how to start acting nice to her."

"Are you afraid she won't be nice back?" Annie laughed. "Oh no, I sound as if I'm talking to one of my eight-year-olds."

"That's okay—I think I've been acting like one," Jennifer said. "I just don't know what to do anymore!"

"Maybe we should try to talk to Nicole—you know, seriously," Annie said. "Or we could do little things to let her know that we care, and that we want to be friends."

"She's really not that bad," Jennifer said. "Once you get past the superior surface stuff, and the 'life is so much better in New York' attitude. She's just different from us, that's all." She shook her head. She never would have imagined that she'd change her mind about Nicole. She wasn't even sure what had caused her to do so.

Out on the field, there was a loud shriek. Jennifer looked over toward the sideline, where Marian had her arms wrapped around Andy's waist. Andy was holding the football, a startled expression on his face.

"It's touch football, not tackle!" Justin yelled at her.

Annie laughed. "Look at Andy's face! He's turning beet-red."

Marian wouldn't let him go. "Finally, I caught you," she said. "I'm not going to let go, no matter what anyone says."

"Oh, yes you are." Andy dropped the ball, then pried her arms from around his waist.

Marian looked as if she wanted to cry. Andy jogged back to his team, which was already gathered in a huddle.

"Can you believe her?" Jennifer said. "I'm not that bold, and I'm four years older than she is.

Doesn't she realize that she's making a fool of herself?"

"Remember when we were thirteen and I fell in love with Skip Nelson, the guy who taught waterskiing?" Annie asked.

"That was different," Jennifer said. "You really liked him."

"And she probably really likes Andy. You can see why a thirteen-year-old would have a crush on him, can't you? He's cute, funny, nice . . . In fact, I'm surprised no one's snatched him up by now," Annie said.

"Like who?" Jennifer asked. "Who do you think would?"

Annie shrugged. "I don't know. Nancy, maybe."

"Nancy? No way. She's not his type," Jennifer said. The thought of Nancy and Andy together was ridiculous.

"Then who is his type?" asked Annie.

"*I* don't know," Jennifer said. "But whoever it is, she's not here!" It was nice that she and Andy had that in common: they had both been trying to find the right person to go out with all summer, and they'd both failed miserably. One of their favorite things to do down on the waterfront, when they had any spare time—and that wasn't often—was to joke about their nonexistent love lives. Jennifer had to keep her sense of humor about the whole thing. If she didn't, she got incredibly bummed out about it.

"Don't look now, but I think Josh is headed this

way," Annie said. He had been standing on the other side of the field, and Jennifer had hoped there'd be so many people between them that he wouldn't notice her.

"I think it's time for me to go into the game," Jennifer said. She ran over to Brett, who was refereeing the game. "Substitution, please." Football wasn't one of her favorite games, but she'd do anything to avoid Josh. So far, he hadn't taken the hint that she wasn't interested. How could people be so blind?

"What's the score, anyway?" Eliot asked after he and Nicole placed their lunch order at Ryan's. After all her attempts to pick out a nice outfit, Nicole hadn't had time to change after the volleyball game. She was still wearing a pair of gray cotton shorts that had rapidly deteriorated since she'd arrived at camp and a white T-shirt with the sleeves rolled up.

"You're asking me?" Nicole said. "Actually, I think the gray team is catching up. We've won practically everything today."

" 'We'?" Eliot said. "So now you're taking the credit for it?" He grinned. "You did make a couple of great spikes in the game."

Nicole felt herself blush. Volleyball was one of the few sports she could stand—she'd had it in gym class in prep school. But Eliot's compliment embarrassed her. She didn't know what it was, but being with Eliot made her nervous. Her hands felt clammy, and she wiped them on her shorts under the table. She kept wondering what Eliot thought of her. Did he like her? Did he think she was boring? If only they were back in New York, they could go to a dance club or a movie, find some diversion. Here, it was only the two of them. No one was playing any music on the jukebox. The windows were open, and all you could hear were birds and an occasional car passing by.

"So," she said, fiddling with the silverware on the table.

" 'So,' " Eliot repeated, "I'm glad Brett said it was okay for us to do this. He's a pretty cool guy, you know."

Nicole nodded. "Cooler than Mara, that's for sure. She'll probably freak out when Brett tells her he gave us his permission."

"Kind of makes you feel like a little kid, having to ask people if you can do stuff, doesn't it?" Eliot laughed.

"Yeah, it does," Nicole agreed. She took a sip from her water glass, then looked around the restaurant. She had no idea what to say next. What if they ran out of things to talk about? Then Eliot would really think she was boring. *I can't believe how nervous I feel!* she thought.

"You said you had a lot on your mind yesterday. Do you want to talk about any of it?" Eliot smiled at her. "No pressure."

Nicole glanced up at him. She still couldn't

decide whether or not to trust Eliot. He was more likely to understand her than anyone else at camp. But suppose he turned on her and told everyone what she was thinking of doing—and how she'd lied to all of them?

She decided to risk it. "You know how I haven't exactly loved being here. Well, I told the other JCs that my mother was coming Sunday, to take me away with her. Actually, that was what I wanted her to do. But when I called her this week to ask her . . ." Nicole's voice trailed off.

"She said no?"

Nicole nodded. "So now I have to admit that I made the whole thing up. But I can't! I mean, it's so embarrassing that your parents don't care enough about you to come rescue you, even when you tell them you're desperate."

Eliot was quiet for a minute. He pushed his hair out of his eyes, and Nicole tried not to stare at him. For the first time, it struck her that she really cared about his opinion. Not only did she think what he had to say would be worthwhile, but she also wanted to know what he thought about *her.* "I think you should tell them," he said. "I don't think you have a choice."

"They're going to laugh at me," Nicole said.

"You just told *me* about it, and I didn't laugh," Eliot said. "I think a lot of people have parents who aren't so understanding. They know how it feels to ask for something and not get it. Were you seriously going to do it?" he asked.

"Sure," Nicole said. "I mean, I didn't have anything to stick around for. I'd much rather spend the summer traveling around—"

"With the same parents who wouldn't come, even when you begged them?" Eliot said.

Nicole frowned. "You make it sound as if they hate me."

"Of course they don't," Eliot said. "I just meant—why would spending time with them be better than hanging out here? Anyway, wasn't it their idea for you to come here?"

Nicole nodded. "Yeah, and I'm going to make them pay for that one."

"You sound like someone in *The Godfather*," Eliot said. "Are you really out for revenge?"

It did sound kind of silly, when Eliot put it that way. "Probably not," Nicole said. "They're just so—unreasonable sometimes, but they think they're being *perfectly* reasonable."

"Like it made perfect sense to them to send you here, even though you said no," Eliot said. "That's typical. And parents can never admit they were wrong, either. That's why they wouldn't come get you, probably."

"Okay, but what am I supposed to say to everyone? I was just joking? They already hate me," Nicole said.

"They hate you? I doubt that."

"Well, they do," Nicole said. "I think they were excited when I told them I was leaving."

Eliot shook his head. "No way."

"Well, I might leave anyway," Nicole said. She hadn't meant to tell Eliot about her plan, but it had slipped out.

"How?" Eliot asked. "What do you mean?"

"I could take the bus down to Boston, then catch the train to New York," Nicole said. The truth was, though, that she didn't have quite enough money for that plan anymore. She'd spent almost all her summer allowance so far. And she couldn't very well ask Mara for an advance on her pay. "Or I could just hitch."

"Hitch? Are you crazy? And anyway, your mother isn't there," Eliot said. "What will you do? You can't just show up without a place to stay."

"I have a couple of friends. I could stay with one of them until my mother comes back from Arizona."

Eliot shook his head again. "I don't get it. You'd rather leave than admit you made up a story? Why are you so obsessed with leaving?"

"Because I feel so boxed in here," Nicole said. "People don't make any effort to be friends with me—"

"Hold on," said Eliot. "Doesn't this count as an effort?"

"Yes," Nicole said. Truthfully, she wasn't that sure she wanted to leave, now that she and Eliot were getting to know each other. The more she knew him, the more she liked him, and—she almost hated to admit it to herself—she really hoped he liked her back. She was definitely developing a major crush on him. Suddenly she noticed she had little butterflies in her stomach, and she found herself wishing Eliot would reach out across the table and touch her.

But as much as she liked Eliot, she didn't know if she could take three more weeks of being cooped up in the Shack with people who didn't care whether she stayed or left. Until just now, she had had it all worked out: she was going to leave on Sunday, no matter what. By Monday, she'd be in another town, with Camp Kissamee far behind, just a distant place in her memory.

Now she wasn't sure she wanted it all to end so soon. She was just beginning to like camp. She enjoyed her cabin, and working on the water, and spending time with Eliot. But she had to leave, to prove a point—to Jennifer and the other JCs who gave her a hard time; to her parents, who acted as if she didn't exist; and to herself—that she could only put up with so much. She deserved better.

The waiter brought their food, and she and Eliot ate in silence for a few minutes. Suddenly, he reached across the table and put his hand over hers. "Listen, Nicole, don't go. I don't want you to leave."

A shiver ran up Nicole's spine. She was afraid to look at him—afraid that if she did, she would start to cry. Eliot was so sweet . . . she couldn't believe it. She didn't deserve someone as nice as he.

Eliot cleared his throat and sat back in his seat, releasing her hand. "Well, I guess we should eat. I told Brett we'd be back by one."

Nicole nodded.

"Are you going to eat that salad or just rearrange it?" Eliot asked.

Nicole smiled and glanced up at him. "I'm not that hungry. I guess I should eat, though. I might have to swim across Torch Lake for the Comps or something."

Eliot started to laugh, and Nicole felt herself relax. She couldn't give Eliot an answer about whether she would stay. The way things stood now, she was leaving—but for Eliot, she would consider staying. It would be embarrassing, but she could tell everyone in the Shack the truth. Maybe it *wasn't* too late to change her mind.

Saturday at lunch inside the Lodge, Mara got up to announce the Comps scores. "The blue team has eighty-five points. And the gray team has . . . Are you ready?" She paused for dramatic effect. "One hundred and two!"

Wild cheers came from the gray team scattered throughout the dining hall. "All right!" Megan cried. Even Nicole felt a small smile creep across her face.

"Don't forget. We still have one full day of competition left. This afternoon we'll have the big water relays: kayaking, canoeing, sailing, and swim meets.

There's plenty of time for the blue team to regain the lead."

"Great," Jennifer muttered, crossing her arms. "I knew I blew it when I let Charlie tackle me in Capture the Flag. That one mistake cost us the game."

"Don't worry," Annie said with a smile. "There's always swimming. You should clean up there."

"You guys make it sound like life and death," Nicole joked, trying to get them to relax. "It's just the Camp Comps."

Jennifer stared at her. "Just the Camp Comps? Oh, I suppose that nobody in Manhattan would be caught dead doing anything so *childish*."

Nicole bit her lip. Did she really say things like that? She remembered Eliot's comment, that she had never given camp a chance. She'd only been trying to get Jennifer to lighten up, but she'd taken it the wrong way. "I just think you're getting too worked up over nothing," she said.

"Like the Comps are nothing," Jennifer grumbled. "It's only one of the most fun things all summer."

"Don't pay any attention to her," Annie said, smiling at Nicole. "She always acts like this when she loses."

"Speaking of losing, the junior-counselor competition starts pretty soon, doesn't it?" Megan asked.

Annie nodded. "And we all get to make idiots of ourselves."

"How does it work?" Nicole asked.

"It's a competition with all kinds of funny games and contests," Lisa explained. "At the end, Tim and Cathy give out an award, but it's really based on other things, too."

"I can't believe Comps will be all over by tomorrow," Megan said.

"That reminds me—your mother's coming tomorrow, right, Nicole? I'm dying to meet her," Beth said. "I bet she's incredibly sophisticated. Which car do you think she'll bring?"

"It depends." The image of her mother's plush green Jaguar didn't give Nicole the same feeling of elation that it might have a few weeks ago. She thought about her conversation with Eliot the day before. She still didn't know what she was going to do, but for now, she decided to stick to her story. She just couldn't bring herself to tell everyone the truth yet. "She's coming tomorrow at noon. I talked to her this morning, and it's all set."

Jennifer's eyes widened. "She's really coming to get you? Have you told Mara yet?"

"No, I'm waiting for the right moment," Nicole said calmly.

"Are you serious?" Lisa asked. "Come on, Nicole, tell me you're joking. You're not going to desert me like that, are you? Whom am I supposed to talk to in the middle of the night when the crickets are keeping me awake?"

Nicole looked at Lisa who, despite everything, had been a fairly loyal friend. She seemed sad at the prospect of Nicole's leaving, even after the rotten way Nicole had sometimes treated her. "I'm still thinking about it," she said. "I might change my mind." She could see Eliot on the other side of the room, laughing with Michael and Gil at their table. Running away from Camp Kissamee meant running away from him.

Suddenly, there was a cry from the middle of the dining room. "Blues against the grays!" a boy shouted. He was standing on a table holding a half-eaten sandwich.

"What's he talking about?" asked Megan.

A second later, the sandwich went flying across the room and landed on another camper's head with a loud *smack*!

"Food fight!" dozens of campers yelled at once as they clambered to their feet and grabbed whatever food they had.

Nicole ducked under the table just as a bowl of Jell-O cubes hurtled through the air. Jennifer, Annie, and Lisa had already dived for the floor. "I didn't know this was part of the Comps," Nicole said.

Jennifer burst out laughing. "Now *that* would be a fun event!"

"Can you see Mara going for that?" Annie added, laughing, too.

"Sure, she'd just wear her yellow slicker," Nicole said. "She hardly ever takes that thing off. Have you noticed?"

"I guess we're supposed to stop them from doing this," said Lisa, "but I'm not moving until they run out of food."

"Hey, look at it this way—someone finally found a good use for Wally's food!" Nicole said, starting to giggle.

They were all laughing so hard that they didn't notice Mara standing over them. She stuck her head underneath the table. "Girls, this is no place to be during a food fight. I expect you to man your positions and restore order."

That only made everyone laugh even harder. Nicole was laughing so hard her stomach hurt. *It's been a long time since I laughed this much,* she thought. This was how she'd pictured camp when she'd thought about what it would take to make it better— getting along with her cabinmates, banding together against Mara, laughing at the campers' antics.

Maybe camp *was* finally getting better. Did that mean it was time to tell everyone the truth?

# CHAPTER
## TWELVE

"Something's wrong with Mimi. I think the other kids have really been picking on her," Katy told Nicole when she showed up at the cabin after lunch. They still had an hour's rest before the water activities would begin.

Nicole was surprised by Katy's tone. She sounded genuinely upset and less clinical than usual. "Why, what's happened?" she asked.

Katy pulled Nicole aside and whispered, "I'm not sure, exactly. You know she bunks with Janet. Well, this morning she was crying, and she wouldn't tell me why." Katy frowned. "It sounds as if they're pressuring her about something, but when I asked her, she just clammed up. I was thinking maybe you could talk to her about it. Of the three of us, she seems to relate best to you."

Nicole nodded. She went over to Mimi's bed and sat down. "You okay?"

"Of course she's okay," Janet replied from the top bunk. "She's just resting and getting ready for our canoe race this afternoon."

Nicole looked up at Janet. "I thought you were on the blue team."

"I am," Janet said. "And this afternoon, I get to race against Mimi. It's going to be *so* hard."

Across the room, Zoe and Marian giggled. "Quiet," Dee warned them. "This is rest hour, remember?"

"So, how's it going?" Nicole asked Mimi quietly. "Did you get nailed with any Jell-O at the food fight?"

Mimi smiled. "No, I ducked."

"Me, too," said Nicole. "Pretty gross, huh?" She made a face. "What's Janet talking about, anyway?"

Mimi looked away. "She just wants to beat me in the canoe race, so their team will win," she whispered.

"But you're not going to let her, are you?" asked Nicole. "You have to try to win for our team. 'Today's the day for grays!'—remember?" Someone had chanted that slogan that morning during the football game, and she hadn't been able to get it out of her mind since. She had to admit that some of the Comps stuff was sort of fun. The campers' excitement was rubbing off on her.

Mimi nodded, still staring at the wall.

"You'd tell me if it was anything more than that, wouldn't you?" asked Nicole. She sensed that Mimi was still holding something back.

"Yes," Mimi said.

"Okay, well, I want you to paddle as hard as you

144

can," Nicole said. "And I'll be watching you—I'm judging that race, you know. So you'd better not give up." Nicole couldn't believe how rah-rah she sounded, but she had to let Mimi know she cared about her and wanted her to do well. That was her job. Mara had told them that their first night—counselors were supposed to act *in loco parentis,* which meant "in the place of parents."

Nicole smiled. If she were acting in the place of *her* parents, her role would be to run off now, to do something else. Instead she sat on the floor just below Mimi's bunk and started to read a magazine. If Mimi wanted to talk, she would be there. That was the best she could do.

By two o'clock, everyone at camp had assembled on the beach and was listening as Justin laid out the plans for the water races. The ropes had been removed from the swimming area, and new areas were set up for Comps contests. Sailing races would take place way out in the middle of the lake, where the sailors would have to navigate their way out to a buoy and then back to the starting point. Jennifer and Nancy were supervising the sailing races from a small motorboat. Swimming relays were being held near one dock, and Nicole would be judging canoe races with Andy on the other. There would be three campers in each canoe, and they'd have to start on the shore, paddle out to a buoy past the dock, and then get back to shore and out of the boat before they could be declared finished. Each winning group would score five points for their team.

The first few races went smoothly. Nicole blew the whistle for them to start, and she and Andy kept track of the canoes in the water. There was so much going on that Nicole didn't have time to think about whether or not she was really leaving the next day. Some of the races were close—and, she had to admit, they were exciting!

When it was Mimi's turn to race, she climbed into a canoe with a boy named Jamie Dixon from Boys' Thirteen and a girl named Lindy, from Girls' Twelve. Their opponents were Marian, Zoe, and Janet. Nicole thought Mimi could almost have a winning edge—if those three started talking, or if Marian caught sight of Andy up on the dock.

Zoe shouted something at Mimi, who didn't answer. *I wish they'd stop teasing her*, Nicole thought. She was going to have to have a talk with them.

"Ouch!" Andy cried. He was hopping around on one foot.

"What happened?" asked Nicole.

"I just got a mammoth splinter from the dock. I need to run down to the boathouse and grab some tweezers from the first-aid kit. I'll be back in two seconds. Can you keep an eye on everything here?"

"Sure," Nicole said. "I'll start the race, and you'll be back before they're finished to call the winners." She hid a smile when she heard Marian shrieking

Andy's name as he limped down the long dock toward the shore.

"Andy, are you all right?" Marian yelled.

"I'm fine!" he called back to her, hurrying off the dock.

"She wants to kiss it and make it better!" Jamie yelled. Marian splashed water on him with her paddle.

"Okay, you guys, calm down. It's time to start this thing!" Nicole yelled. "Are you ready?"

"Ready!" Zoe hollered back. "Are you ready, Mimi?"

"Ready," Mimi answered, much more softly.

"Okay. When I blow the whistle, *go.*" Nicole shaded her eyes with her hand, then blew the whistle. In a flash, the campers jumped into the canoes and started furiously paddling away from shore. *That's weird,* Nicole thought, squinting at Mimi's canoe. It looked as though Mimi wasn't wearing a life jacket. She couldn't tell for sure because Mimi was crouched down in the middle, with Lindy and Jamie on either side of her. Nicole knew Mimi would never get in a canoe without one, though, especially because she wasn't a strong swimmer. She had shown some improvement during the two lessons that Nicole had given her, but she was still uncomfortable in the water.

Nicole wished she hadn't left her sunglasses in her bag at the other end of the dock. The sun was pretty intense, and she was getting a headache from squinting so much. On top of that, she simply couldn't see clearly, with the sunlight reflecting off the dancing blue water. She glanced longingly back at her beach bag. It would only take a second to grab her glasses and get back. She looked out at the canoes. They were out near the buoy; Mimi's was trailing Zoe's by a few feet. By the time they circled the buoy, Nicole would be back.

She dashed down the dock, rummaged in her bag, and grabbed her sunglasses. She slid them onto her nose and felt her eye muscles relax. *Much better*, she told herself as she started to jog back down the dock.

That was when she heard the scream.

It all seemed to happen in slow motion. She saw the blue team's canoe crash into the gray team's canoe, just as they turned around the buoy. The canoe that Mimi was in pitched to one side, and Mimi slid headfirst into the water—without a life vest on! Jamie and Lindy fell in after her.

Nicole froze. For the first time in her life she knew how it felt to be too scared to move. She saw Andy race past her onto the dock, yelling something. Justin was chasing along after him. The cheers and cries from the crowd on the beach were silenced.

"Help her!" Nicole cried, suddenly finding the strength to run down the dock. "Mimi!"

"She doesn't know how to swim!" Zoe yelled.

Justin and Andy were already in the water. The canoe was bobbing upside down on the surface of the lake. Several feet away, Lindy popped up in her orange life vest, then Jamie. But Mimi was nowhere to be seen.

Justin and Andy made it to the end of the dock and jumped in. They swam frantically toward the overturned canoe. When they got there, Andy took a deep breath and dove underwater.

He quickly came back to the surface, gasping. "I can't find her," he said in a panicky voice.

Then Justin took over. He did a quick dive and disappeared under the canoe. "I've got her," he shouted, coming up after a horrifying minute. "Somebody call an ambulance!"

The dock filled up as people rushed out to see what was happening. Because everyone in camp had been down at the lake, it didn't take long for a large crowd to form. Tim, Cathy, and Mara were there, and Brett took off for the Lodge to call the hospital.

"Everyone—back off, we need room," Tim said, clearing a circle. Justin was swimming toward the dock, his arm crooked around Mimi's chest. She was half floating in his arms, her face pale white.

"She's unconscious. She must have hit her head on the side of the canoe when she fell in," Justin said tersely as Tim and Andy helped him up onto the dock. Nicole watched it all as if she were inside a nightmare. Justin knelt over Mimi's body with one hand on her neck, feeling for a pulse. Then he began to administer mouth-to-mouth resuscitation.

*Don't let anything happen to her. Don't let her die, please*, Nicole prayed. This was all her fault. If anything happened to Mimi, she'd be the one to blame. *Why didn't she tell me what they were up to? I would have taken care of her.*

"Her heart's beating," Justin said, looking up for a second. "It's faint, but it's beating."

Marian and Zoe both burst into tears. They had pulled their canoe in and climbed up onto the dock with Janet. All three of them were standing behind Cathy, as pale as ghosts themselves.

"It's my fault," Marian choked out. "We dared her . . . not to wear a life jacket."

Andy whirled around, furious. "How could you do something like that? You know the rules around here!"

"We'll deal with that later, Andy," Tim said sternly.

For a full minute no one said a word. Everyone was waiting and watching for Mimi to regain consciousness. Finally, her eyelids flickered a few times, and she slowly opened her eyes.

Justin sat back and ran the back of his hand over his forehead. "She's going to be okay. She'll probably have a major headache, but she's all right."

Mimi moved her fingers a little, and Nicole felt enormous waves of relief wash over her. *She's okay,* she thought. Nicole wasn't, though—she felt as if she was going to faint.

Eliot came over and stood next to Nicole. He reached out to take her hand, and she squeezed his. "She'll be fine," he said softly. Nicole nodded.

"Now," Tim said, looking around at the circle of faces, "who was on guard here? Who was judging the canoe races?"

"Andy and Nicole," Justin said.

"I had a huge splinter in my foot, and I went to the boathouse to grab the tweezers. I asked Nicole to watch for me," Andy said.

"Andy's right, it was my fault." Nicole's voice trembled. "I . . . I don't know what I was thinking. I needed my sunglasses, and I thought I could get back . . ." Eliot squeezed her hand in support, and she felt as if she was going to start crying.

"You *never* leave a lifeguard post," Tim said. This was the first time Nicole had ever heard him sound so severe. "Nicole, Andy, we'll see you back in our office as soon as we get Mimi to the hospital." He turned to the girls in Nicole's cabin. "Tell me again what happened."

"She . . . uh . . ." Marian said in a whisper, wiping away a tear. "We've been teasing her . . ."

"It was my idea," Zoe interrupted in a quiet voice, as the circle of campers leaned closer to hear. "We knew she wasn't that good a swimmer. We got her to promise not to wear a life vest, and we distracted Andy and Nicole by splashing and shouting so they wouldn't see. We told Mimi she had to lose the race for her team. We knew she'd be afraid to go fast if she wasn't wearing a life jacket."

"But we never thought she'd fall in! It was a complete accident!" Janet cried. "We just wanted them to lose. We almost died when we saw her canoe tip over."

"I'd like to see all three of you in the office as well," Cathy said. "This is an extremely serious incident. We're lucky Mimi wasn't hurt—we're all lucky." Her gaze took in the whole circle, but Nicole felt it linger on her.

She knew she was more to blame than anybody else. She should have made absolutely sure that everyone was wearing life vests. She should have waited to start the race until after she had gotten her sunglasses. Once Andy was gone, she should have watched twice as hard as she normally would have.

*Should have,* Nicole thought. Because she hadn't done what she should have, Mimi had almost drowned. *Some counselor I make. I don't even deserve to be here.*

# CHAPTER
## THIRTEEN

Nicole had a sinking feeling in her stomach as she walked up the long hill from the lake toward the main office in the lodge with Mara and Andy. In her head, she kept going over and over the scene down at the lake. Marian's cry, the canoe tipping over, the horrible moment when Lindy and Jamie bobbed to the surface . . . and Mimi didn't. How could she have let Mimi leave the dock without her life jacket? How could she have run back like that when there wasn't *anyone* on the dock to watch?

*Just let Mimi be okay*, she kept repeating to herself. *If she's okay, nothing else matters.*

Still, she dreaded the scene that she knew was coming. Tim and Cathy were going to have to lay into her.

Andy seemed to be thinking the same thing. "We're in for it," he whispered when Mara moved ahead of them, like a prison warden escorting them to their cells.

"You're not in trouble. You left me in charge. I'm the one who's responsible," Nicole said.

Andy shook his head. "No, I shouldn't have left, either."

Nicole glanced over at him. She hadn't been very nice to Andy. She'd walked all over him, treating him as if he didn't have any feelings. Had she really been that self-absorbed, so obsessed about getting Gil to like her? And now, when Andy could really get back at her, he was being nice. It made her wince.

Tim and Cathy arrived from the hospital about ten minutes later and quickly ushered Andy and Nicole into their office. "Sit down," Tim said. His voice sounded much more solemn than usual, and Nicole felt a moment of blind panic. What if . . .

"Mimi's fine," Tim said abruptly. "She's shaken up, but otherwise okay. The doctors want her to stay overnight, just to make sure she gets a good night's rest."

Nicole let out a huge sigh of relief.

Cathy signaled for Mara to take a seat. "Nicole, Andy, this isn't an easy thing for us to talk about. In the fifteen years since we have been in charge of Camp Kissamee, we've never had an incident like this. You can imagine how upset we are."

"It wasn't Andy's fault." Nicole was shocked to hear those words come out of her mouth, but she knew it was the right thing to say. "He left me in charge, and I don't think he should get into trouble."

Andy stared at her, looking amazed. Mara seemed surprised as well, but Cathy paid no attention to Nicole's remarks. "Andy, can you tell us what happened this afternoon?" she asked.

Andy explained the sequence of events. "I came back as quickly as I could. By that time, the kids were screaming and Mimi was in the water," he concluded.

"Did you see her go out without a life preserver?" Tim asked.

Andy shook his head. "No. There was so much going on, everything happened so fast . . . I guess we just sort of assumed that the kids knew the rules."

"Mimi was in the middle of the canoe," Nicole added. "Once Jamie and Lindy got in, it was impossible to see her."

Tim and Cathy glanced at each other, then Cathy turned back to Andy. "In the future, you should remember that it's ultimately *your* responsibility to make sure campers follow the rules, not theirs."

"Okay, I'll remember," Andy mumbled, his head down.

"Good." Cathy put both hands on the table. "That's all, Andy."

He glanced at Nicole. "But—"

"That's all," Tim said sternly. Andy slowly got to his feet, and Nicole felt her pulse quicken. She watched Andy close the door noiselessly behind him, and she tried to swallow. Her throat felt as dry as paper.

"Nicole, under the circumstances, Cathy and I

feel that the responsibility for Mimi's accident rests in your hands, not Andy's. True, you both shared responsibility for making sure the campers were all wearing life vests. Let's just assume, for the moment, that that was a legitimate oversight. I can believe that the kids tricked you somehow. But the fact remains that Andy left the dock only because he knew you were still there to watch. And then *you* left. With no one else to back you up. That's an unpardonable error in judgment, Nicole."

Nicole stared at the floor in front of their big oak desk. Tim was right. What she had done was unforgivable.

"Maybe you'd like to say something," Cathy said calmly.

Nicole shook her head, tears filling her eyes. "There isn't much I can say, except . . . I'm sorry. I don't know what I was thinking. It was completely irresponsible of me . . . you're right."

Tim put the tips of his fingers together and swiveled slowly in his chair. "As we said, we've never had an incident like this before. We're not entirely comfortable with our decision, but we feel we're going to have to let you go."

"But—" Nicole began to protest, but Cathy cut her off.

"I'm sorry," she said. "We really can't see any other way to handle this situation. I know it hasn't been easy for you here, and, as a matter of fact, we've heard from some people, Mara in particular,

156

who've found that it's been difficult to deal with you. We've tried to set their complaints aside, because we know you're new here. But after something like this, well . . . we have to take those complaints a little more seriously. Given the severity of today's accident, and the way it happened, I'm not sure we'd feel confident trusting you again. We need to have absolute trust in our staff," Cathy concluded.

Nicole dug her fingernails into the arm of her chair to keep herself from crying. She couldn't believe her ears. They were letting her go. Firing her. After all those weeks when she had wanted to leave, she'd made it through. Now, it wasn't up to her. They didn't want *her* around.

"We'll call your parents if you'd like," Tim said, glancing through a manila folder on his desk. "Since your mother's out west, maybe your father—"

"No!" Nicole cried. It would be a total disaster if they called her father and told him she was being fired. For once, she was grateful that he was out of the country. They probably wouldn't reach him even if they tried. "I mean, I'd much rather call them myself," she said.

"Of course." Cathy nodded. "Go ahead, Nicole. Call them, sort out the arrangements. We can speak to them when they arrive."

Nicole stared at her index finger. She'd been gripping the chair so hard, one of her nails had broken off. A few weeks ago, leaving Camp Kissamee had seemed like a great idea. Up until a few hours ago, she had still been considering it. Who was going to come get her? A tear slid down her cheek, and she hastened to wipe it away, hoping no one would notice.

Cathy got up and put her arm around Nicole's shoulders. "Believe me, I know how hard this must be. Tim and I wouldn't have made this decision unless we felt we had to. We believe this is the best solution. Do you agree?"

Nicole couldn't answer her. Until today, she'd never intended to stay at Camp Kissamee. She'd hated it from day one. If they had fired her two weeks ago, even five days ago, she would have been only too happy to walk out, head held high.

But not now. Not now that she was beginning to feel as though she belonged. Deep down, she knew that she belonged here more than she did anywhere else—with people who actually seemed to care about her.

*At least they used to*, Nicole thought, rising to leave the office. Once everyone knew she'd been fired, they would probably go back to hating her as much as they had before.

"What do you think happened?" Jennifer asked, swinging her legs back and forth as she sat on her bunk looking down at Annie.

"Jen, if you ask me that one more time, I'm going to kill you," Annie said. "I don't know what happened!"

"I still can't believe it, if those kids were telling the truth," Lisa said. "I mean, I have some bullies in my cabin, too, but they'd never do anything deliberately to jeopardize someone's life." She shook her head. "It was so scary when I saw Justin come out of the water, holding her like that . . ."

"I know," Megan said. "All I could think of was—what if he doesn't make it to her in time?"

Jennifer kept swinging her legs back and forth. The rhythmic motion was soothing to her. She couldn't imagine what Andy must be feeling right now. Down at the waterfront, where she had coached swimming and lifeguarded almost every day, the thought of seeing someone almost drown had been a daily fear during her first few days. But after a while, she had let go of that fear, beginning to trust the kids in the water as well as her ability to watch them at all times. If anyone had ever gone under the way Mimi had, Jennifer didn't know if she would have been able to react as quickly as Justin had. That thought scared her.

But she hadn't been responsible for the kids in the canoe race. Nicole and Andy had been. Jennifer knew Andy must be feeling terrible about his part in the accident. Despite some of her misgivings about Nicole, she knew that Nicole must be suffering a tremendous amount of guilt, too.

"Tim and Cathy must be having quite a talk with them," Beth said. "It's been at least an hour since they went into the Lodge!"

Everyone at camp had been sent back to their cabins following the accident. The Comps would be finished the next day, if at all. No one seemed to mind. It was obvious that there were some things that were much more important than a camp competition. Mara had asked the JCs to go back to their cabins and talk to Nicole and Andy, to offer them their support. You had to say one thing about Mara, Jennifer thought: even though she could be a royal pain, she was pretty sensitive about helping people deal with painful situations.

The back door to the Shack opened, and everyone looked at one another with nervous glances. "Nicole, is that you?" Beth called.

"Yes," came a muffled reply.

"We're really sorry about what happened," Lisa said as Nicole wandered into the front part of the cabin. "Are you okay?"

Nicole didn't look okay to Jennifer. Her usually neat hair was all messy, and her eyes were pink, as if she had been crying. Jennifer felt so bad. She didn't know what to say. Even if Nicole had been partly responsible for the accident, it was obvious that she was really suffering because of it.

"Did you talk to Tim and Cathy about what happened?" Annie asked.

Nicole stared at a spot on the floor. "Yeah, I talked to them. Actually, they talked to *me*." She paused. She seemed to be thinking something over for a minute. Then she said, "They think I should leave camp. So, I'm leaving." She had the same old nonchalant voice, but it was quavering a little.

"'Leaving'?" Megan repeated.

"They're making you leave?" Lisa was dumbfounded.

"I don't believe it!" Jennifer cried.

"Yeah, well, it's no big deal. I was leaving anyway, remember?" Nicole glanced up at Jennifer.

Jennifer couldn't read her expression. Was she glad to be leaving—or was she just bluffing her way through this?

"So what are you going to do? Is your mom still coming tomorrow?" asked Beth.

"No." Nicole chewed on her lower lip. "I'm going to . . . meet her at the airport in Boston. She's flying in from Tucson, and since I won't be sticking around, we decided to spend the rest of the summer visiting my father in France and traveling around. We'll just leave from Boston tomorrow night."

No one said anything for a minute. Then Annie said, "That sounds like a fun way to finish the summer."

Nicole seemed to be regaining her composure. She pulled her hair back from her face and ran her fingers through it to make it neater. "It'll be great," she said. "I can't wait to see Paris. Of course, I will have to get over the pain of not going on that hayride."

*Typical Nicole*, thought Jennifer. *She never misses a chance to get her digs in.*

"But, Nicole—couldn't you say anything to convince them to let you stay?" Lisa asked. "I don't want you to leave." Apparently it hadn't struck Lisa that Nicole *wanted* to leave, Jennifer thought. Lisa obviously hadn't believed her earlier comments about taking off for the rest of the summer.

"Come on, Lisa, it won't be that bad," Nicole said. "You'll have a great summer whether I'm here or not."

Lisa shook her head. "It won't be the same."

"No, you'll have a lot more room in here, for one thing," Nicole joked.

Lisa managed a weak smile.

"Well, I've got to get my suitcases out of the storage loft in the Barn," Nicole said. "See you guys later. Just think, tonight will be my last dinner at this place!" She breezed out the front door with the same self-confidence as always.

"She seems to be taking it pretty well," Annie said.

"I don't know," said Megan. "It seemed as though maybe she's taking it *too* well."

"What do you mean?" Lisa asked.

"I think she's dying inside. It's just an act," Megan said.

"She is a good actress," Beth admitted. "And there's no way she'd let us know how she was really feeling."

"Look, I know a lot of you guys can't stand Nicole. I know you complain about her a lot. But I like her,"

Lisa said. "Even though she walked all over me when she first got here, she's . . . well . . . she's changed, or something. I mean, she's starting to relax. She hasn't given me a hard time about anything in a long time. Even though she's not the easiest person to have as a roommate, I'm really going to miss her."

Megan laughed. "Me, too. I've gotten used to having her around, even if we don't always agree."

"That's the great thing about camp," Beth said. "You end up becoming friends with people who are nothing like you, just because you live together."

Jennifer hopped down from the top bunk. "I never thought I'd hear myself say this, but in her own way Nicole is kind of good to have around. She's entertaining, anyway. I don't think it'll be the same around here without her."

"Dee was telling me in arts and crafts the other day that Nicole has actually made a big contribution to their cabin," Annie said. "When Dee was sick and Nicole stayed there, I guess she was fantastic with the campers."

"She was even doing an okay job on the waterfront, until today," Jennifer said. "That's what Andy told me."

"I wonder . . ." Beth began.

"What?" Lisa and Annie asked at the same time.

"Oh, nothing." Beth shook her head. "It wouldn't make any difference. You heard what she said—she was planning on leaving anyway. She's probably glad this happened. Not that she wanted any harm to come to Mimi—I don't mean that. She's just probably relieved to be getting out of here. There wouldn't be any point in trying to stop her."

"Anyway, if we decided to, there's nothing *we* could do about it," Annie said. "Tim and Cathy made the decision."

Jennifer nodded. Annie was right. Whether Nicole stayed or left wasn't up to them. She was leaving, like it or not. Jennifer just wished she could read Nicole better. Beth and Megan were probably right. She had a feeling Nicole's excitement about seeing Paris was just another one of her acts.

"Annie!" Jennifer leaned out of bed to shake Annie by the shoulder. "Annie, did you hear that?"

"What," Annie mumbled groggily.

"That noise." Jennifer slid down from her bunk and slipped her feet into the sneakers by her bed. She heard the faint knock again. "Someone's at the window. Get up and grab a flashlight. We've got to go out and see what it is."

"It's probably just a raccoon," Annie said, climbing out of bed. She put on her moccasins, grabbed her flashlight from her nightstand, and followed Jennifer outside.

Jennifer swung the beam of the flashlight around from tree to tree.

"Over here!" she heard someone whisper. She spotted Eliot, waving to her from behind a tree.

"Eliot!" Annie exclaimed. "What are you doing here?"

"*Shh.*" He put his finger to his lips, and they made their way toward him. "I don't want Nicole to hear what I have to say. This is urgent."

"It'd better be," Jennifer grumbled. "It's three thirty in the morning!"

"This will just take a minute," Eliot replied. "I had to tell you now because she's planning on leaving tomorrow. I didn't know if I'd get the chance to speak to you privately before then."

"Why all the secrecy, Eliot?" Annie asked, wrapping her arms around her shoulders to ward off the cold night air.

"She'd freak out if she knew what I was telling you. She's been avoiding me ever since the accident today, but I heard from Lisa that Nicole is meeting her mom in Boston tomorrow," Eliot said.

Jennifer and Annie exchanged glances. "So?" Jennifer asked.

"So, she's lying. No one's going to meet her. Her mom is in Tucson, and she wouldn't come to get her when Nicole asked," Eliot said.

"You're kidding," Jennifer said.

"But wouldn't Tim or Cathy have called and told her what happened? Then she'd have to come," Annie reasoned.

Eliot shook his head. "I know what's going on in Nicole's head these days. She's really angry with her parents because neither one of them would take her when she wanted to leave. I'm sure she told Tim and Cathy that *she'd* call them. Her dad's really expecting her to do a good job here. He's not big on people making mistakes. I doubt Nicole would have told him she'd been kicked out."

"So she was making that whole story up, about her mom coming to get her to take her to Paris?" Jennifer asked.

Eliot nodded. "Last I heard, she was planning on catching the bus back to New York and trying to find friends to stay with—or else hitchhiking."

"No way!" Annie's eyes widened. "Hitchhiking? With all that luggage? Anyway, it's dangerous, even up here in rural Vermont. Where's she going to *go*?"

Jennifer sighed. "Imagine having to make things up like that about your parents. She must be pretty lonely."

Eliot scuffed the pine needles on the ground with his bare feet. "I was thinking . . . I don't know if it'll help, but if some of us could talk to Tim and Cathy, maybe get them to rethink their decision to fire her—"

"That's a great idea," Annie said. "If they see how much support she has from the rest of us, it might work."

"Look, I know Nicole's not always easy to get along with, but I've gotten to know her a lot better over the past couple of weeks. Even though she acts as though her life back home is incredibly easy and fun, it isn't. She has problems, just like all of us," Eliot said.

Jennifer nodded. "Okay, we'll help."

"Thanks. See you guys tomorrow," Eliot said. He started walking toward his cabin, and they tiptoed back toward the Shack.

"Wow. I never thought I'd say this," Annie whispered, "but I actually feel sorry for Nicole."

"I know," Jennifer whispered back. "Me, too. What happened today could have happened to any of us. But not to have any place to go. That's really sad. I can't believe her parents are so unsympathetic."

As she climbed back into bed, Jennifer had a sudden vision of Nicole spending the next night . . . where? At a friend's house? At a bus station? Eliot was right. They had to help her.

# CHAPTER
## FOURTEEN

"Are you all right?"

Nicole nodded, helping herself to a bowl of cereal. "I'm fine," she told Dee. "How's Mimi? Has anyone heard about her this morning?"

"She just got back, right as flagpole ended." Dee grinned. "She's trying to fight her way through the hero's welcome the cabin is giving her. They'll be here any second."

Katy reached over and put her hand on Nicole's arm. "Dee and I heard about what Tim and Cathy said to you. We just want you to know we . . . uh . . ." For once, Katy seemed to be out of labels for what she was feeling.

Nicole shrugged. "Don't worry about it. Tim and Cathy made the right decision," she said. She could feel her face turning pink. So everyone knew she was getting kicked out. It was humiliating. "Have the campers heard, too?" she asked.

"Mimi knows. None of the others do," Dee said.

Nicole took a bite of cereal and tried to hold back her tears. By tonight, the whole camp would know.

They'd all be sitting around talking about her and what a rotten counselor she'd been. And she'd be hitchhiking, trying to get back to New York, trying to find somewhere to stay.

At the moment all she wanted was to turn the clock back and make it yesterday at this time. If only she could have another chance . . . but she didn't. She had run out of chances.

The girls in Cabin Thirteen came rushing through the door, then pushed their way through the dining room toward their table. Mimi was in the center of the crowd, the girls around her asking questions like: "Did they make you wear one of those ugly nightgowns?" and "Was the food any better than Wally's?" Mimi answered them patiently, as unfazed by all this attention as she'd been when they had all neglected her earlier in the summer.

"Hi," she said shyly to Nicole. "May I sit next to you?"

Nicole was surprised that Mimi would want to sit at the same table with her, let alone right next to her. She nodded, giving the younger girl a shy smile. Seeing Mimi was even harder than she'd expected. It brought back to her what could have happened—what *almost* happened, she thought.

"How are you feeling?" Nicole managed to ask.

"Okay, I guess," Mimi said. She took a sip of orange juice.

Nicole took a deep breath. Her hands were

shaking. "Mimi, I'm so sorry about what happened yesterday," she said.

"It's okay," Mimi said.

"No, it isn't," Nicole said. "I should have been watching you more closely. Things shouldn't have gone so far. I should have made sure you were wearing your life jacket."

"We're the ones who made her do it," Zoe said. "It's not your fault."

"It *is* my fault," Nicole said. Still, she was glad to hear Zoe take some responsibility. She hoped that she, Marian, and Janet had learned their lesson. She was pretty sure that they would leave Mimi alone for the rest of summer.

Mimi looked up at Nicole. "It was an accident, when the boat tipped over. It's okay, Nicole. I don't blame you."

"Will you at least forgive me?" Nicole asked.

"Of course," Mimi said. "Even though I still don't think you did anything wrong."

"But I did," Nicole insisted. That was why she was getting kicked out. Mimi had to know that, too.

Mimi just looked up at her with sad eyes. Nicole knew what she was thinking. She didn't want Nicole to leave. They had sort of stuck together over the summer. Nicole didn't know how she could face saying good-bye to Mimi after everything that had happened.

"Dee, would it be all right if I took off early?"

Nicole asked. "I have some stuff I have to do back at the Shack."

Dee nodded, and Nicole rose from the table.

"Hey, Nicole, are you going to warm up for the relay?" Casey asked, smiling. "We *have* to win."

At flagpole that morning, Brett had announced that a relay race would be held to determine the winner of Comps. At the moment, the score was tied.

"No way, the blues are going to win," Janet said confidently.

"Uh uh." Lynne shook her head. "All the way with gray!"

Nicole smiled faintly as she walked away from her cabin's table. Chances were that she wouldn't see any of the girls again, but she couldn't bring herself to say good-bye. It was too painful.

"Take a number," Jennifer joked when Eliot came up to join her outside Tim and Cathy's office after breakfast. "Beth's in there now. I've been waiting for twenty minutes. Megan and Lisa are after me. They got tired of waiting, so they went to get a cup of coffee from Wally."

Eliot grinned. "This is great! Do you think it's working?"

"Dee said they seemed to listen to what she and Katy had to say. I guess Mimi talked to them on the way back from the hospital, too. That's what Dee said."

"That's fantastic," Eliot said. "I bet Mimi made quite an impression. Dee's opinion has to carry some weight, too. Wow, Nicole has a whole bunch of people sticking up for her."

"I wouldn't go that far," Jennifer said. "It's just that none of us wants to see another counselor get kicked out. She can be a pain, but she's part of the Shack. We JCs need to stick together."

"You and Annie haven't told anyone what I said to you last night, have you?" Eliot asked, lowering his voice. "About her parents, I mean."

Jennifer shook her head. "We just said we thought it might be a good idea to rally around her, give her some support."

"Good." Eliot pushed his hair out of his eyes and gave her a lopsided grin. "Thanks."

"No problem." Jennifer sighed and leaned against the wall. It was ironic, she thought. A few weeks ago, she would never have believed that she'd be waiting to ask Tim and Cathy to give Nicole another chance. She hadn't given much thought to the fact that Eliot was behind all this yet. She'd noticed that he and Nicole were spending more time together. Was it possible that Eliot was interested in Nicole? she wondered.

The office door opened, and Beth walked out into the hallway.

"How did it go?" Eliot asked eagerly.

"Okay, I guess," Beth said. "I talked, and they

172

listened. I think they're starting to give their decision a second look."

Jennifer took a deep breath and walked into the office. "Are you guys ready for me?"

"Jennifer—this is a surprise," Cathy said. "What did you want to talk to us about?"

"Nicole, of course. What else?" Jennifer replied.

Tim looked confused. "Well, it's just that we know you two haven't been getting along. Did you want to speak in support of her, or against her?"

Had it been that obvious? Jennifer didn't know that her relationship with Nicole was a matter of public knowledge. But at a small camp like Kissamee, everyone seemed to know everyone else's business, sooner or later. "In support," Jennifer said. "Maybe you guys don't know this, but I really do like Nicole. I think she deserves another chance."

"Go on," Cathy prompted, leaning back in her chair.

Jennifer and Annie went back to the Shack after having talked to Tim and Cathy. They still had half an hour to get ready for the big relay race, and they wanted to see how Nicole was doing. "I think we should tell her that Tim and Cathy might change their minds," Annie said.

"I don't," Jennifer said. "Not until they make a decision. If we get her hopes up and it's not true, she'd feel even worse—especially if she found out we all went to bat for her."

Annie pushed open the cabin door, and they walked into the back bedroom. The cabin was empty. "Look, Jen—her bed's been stripped. Her bags are gone, too."

Jennifer stopped short, staring at the bare bed. "It sure looks as though she checked out."

"What if she already left?" Annie cried.

"Don't jump to conclusions," Jennifer said, even though she was thinking the same thing. "Maybe she just moved her suitcases down to the Lodge."

"Hey, look!" Annie grabbed a slip of paper off the floor, near Nicole's bed. "It's a letter. The wind must have blown it off." The two girls read the note together, their shoulders touching.

Jennifer, Annie, Beth, Megan, and Lisa,
Sorry to take off without a good-bye, but I hate that kind of thing. I didn't feel like waiting around to have Griffin take me to the airport. I left some of my stuff at the Lodge, because I didn't feel like carrying it all. But don't worry —I'll arrange to have it shipped once I get back to the city, not that I'll need my camp clothes when I get there. I hope you guys make it through the summer. It's been fun. See you later.

Nicole

"Oh, no!" Annie gasped. "Eliot was right, Jen. She ran off!"

"But she can't have," Jennifer said. "Not when Tim and Cathy might change their minds about letting her stay!"

"We have to find her." Annie folded the note hastily and shoved it in her pocket. "No wonder she left her luggage here—she's hitchhiking. Some maniac could be picking her up right now!"

Lisa opened the back door to the Shack. "What's going on? You guys look upset. Don't be. I just came from—"

"Nicole's gone," Jennifer interrupted her.

"Gone? But Tim just told me he's changed his mind, and they're going to let her stay, on probation."

"Well, she decided not to stick around," Annie said.

"But I thought she wasn't meeting her mother until tonight," Lisa said. "Why did she leave so early?"

"Lisa, she's not meeting her mother," Jennifer said. "Her parents don't even know she's leaving yet." She hadn't intended to betray Nicole's secret, but she knew that the JCs were going to have to organize a search. That meant telling everyone else in the Shack the truth: that Nicole's parents didn't know she'd been kicked out, and that they didn't seem to care what happened to her.

"Why did she say she was, then?" Lisa asked.

"She was lying because she didn't want us to know the truth. She asked her mother to come get her last week, and her mother refused," Jennifer said.

"Wow. Some friend I've been," Lisa said sadly. "I knew all along Nicole wasn't happy here, and lately I've been so wrapped up in Michael and my own life that I hardly even spoke to her. I didn't know things with her folks were that bad."

"Don't be so hard on yourself. None of us has actually made such a great effort to get close to Nicole," Annie said. "But right now, we're the closest thing to family she has."

There was a sharp knock on the front door of the Shack. "Come in!" Jennifer called.

Eliot walked into the cabin, with Tim and Cathy right behind him. "Hi. We came to talk to Nicole," he said in a cheerful voice.

"She's not here," Annie said.

"She left a note. She took off," Lisa explained.

Tim frowned. "I don't understand. I thought Griffin was taking her to the airport this afternoon. Her flight to Boston isn't until four thirty."

"Oh, no," Eliot groaned. "This is exactly what I was afraid of."

"Could someone please explain what's going on?" Cathy demanded.

"She isn't going to Boston," Eliot said. "She's not meeting her mother. Her mother's staying out in Arizona. Her father's in Europe—he travels all the time on business."

"But I thought she was going to travel with them," Cathy said.

"She wishes," Eliot said. "Actually, they both told her they didn't have time for her. Not when she knew she was kicked out—before then, she'd called them because she wanted to leave camp. She was pretty unhappy here, you know."

Tim nodded. "I suspected as much."

"Nicole's not meeting anyone," Eliot said, "because she doesn't have anyone to meet."

"Where is she going, then?" asked Cathy.

"She's got some idea about hitching to New York, trying to find some friends to stay with. But she hasn't gotten in touch with anyone there yet. I think most of her friends are gone for the summer, too."

"We'd better find her before she goes too far," Tim said. "The fact is, Cathy and I came up here to tell Nicole we want to give her another chance. That was before we knew she didn't have anywhere to go."

"Let's go to Middlebrook," Jennifer suggested. "She's only been gone since breakfast. I bet she's still there, trying to get a ride."

"And if she isn't?" asked Lisa. "What if someone already picked her up?"

"It's a rural area. There wouldn't be much traffic this morning," Tim said. "Anyway, don't think that way, Lisa. We'll find her, and she'll be all right."

"Eliot, can you take a few people in your car? We'll go out in the camp van on Route Twenty-eight

—you try Route Seventeen and Main Street," Cathy said. "We'll meet back here later."

Eliot nodded. "Who wants to come?"

Five minutes later, Annie, Jennifer, and Lisa piled into Eliot's Honda. "At least it's not raining," Eliot said. "It'll make it easier to see her."

"I hate myself for being such a lousy friend," Lisa complained from the backseat.

"How do you think I feel?" Jennifer said. "I'm the one who gave her the hardest time."

"Well, in all fairness, she deserved it sometimes," Annie reminded her.

"That's true," Eliot said. "I did my fair share of teasing her, but she always came right back."

"Maybe, but I didn't have to be on her case all the time," Jennifer said. Sitting in the front seat, she watched the familiar scenery flash by. On the way past the camp gates, she noticed that someone had recently crossed out the *a* and the last *e* on the camp sign so that it read "Camp Kiss Me." Even that didn't make Jennifer smile. She was too worried.

They turned left at the camp gates and headed out onto the road that would take them into town. Jennifer stared straight ahead at the road. She was trying to imagine how friendless Nicole felt right now, all alone, running away.

She saw something up ahead that looked as if it could be a person. *It's probably just a cow trying to cross the road,* she thought. Thinking about cows reminded her of the way Nicole called Middlebrook

Hicksville all the time. She said she'd never lived anywhere where there were more cows than people.

"Hey, look!" Eliot suddenly cried. He pointed ahead of them. "There she is!"

Sure enough, it was Nicole, standing a hundred yards or so in front of them, holding out her thumb and looking bored.

"I'm surprised she doesn't have a sign in her hand that says 'New York City or Bust!'" Annie joked as they pulled closer.

Eliot drove the car over onto the shoulder, and they climbed out. "Going somewhere?" he asked, walking up to her.

Nicole had her sunglasses on, and she peered over the top of them at the group as they approached her. "What are you doing here? I told you I can't stand sappy good-byes."

"We didn't come to say good-bye," Eliot said. "We came to take you back."

Nicole stared at him. "Take me back? What do you mean?"

"Tim and Cathy are out looking for you, too. They changed their minds," Annie said, stepping closer. "Nicole, listen—"

"Oh, come on. *You* don't want me to come back," Nicole said bitterly. "None of you do." She didn't look at Eliot.

"Yes, we do!" Lisa protested. "We need you back in our cabin."

Nicole still didn't look convinced.

"Look, Nicole, maybe you and I don't see everything eye to eye. But I'd miss you if you left. I know everyone else would, too," Jennifer said. She waited anxiously for Nicole's reply.

Before Nicole could say anything, the camp van pulled up on the other side of the road. Tim and Cathy climbed out, followed by Beth and Megan.

"Nicole!" Cathy cried, looking both ways before jogging across the road. "We're so glad to see you!"

"So are we," Megan said, smiling.

"Have they told you yet? We'd like you to stay," Tim said.

"Why?" Nicole asked bluntly. "I thought it was a cut-and-dried case. After all, I was the one to blame for Mimi's accident. And I haven't been much of a junior counselor," she added.

Tim cleared his throat. "We had our worries," he said quietly. "But this morning we started to hear another side of the story. First Mimi talked to us. Then Dee and Katy came to see us. Then your cabinmates. They all had the same thing to say. They don't want to see you go."

Nicole looked dumbfounded. "My cabinmates?" She glanced around the circle at everybody.

"Come back, Nicole. Stay at camp," Lisa begged. "We really want you to."

Nicole was quiet. Jennifer couldn't imagine what was going on in her mind. Would she really want to leave camp, headed for nowhere—when she could stay with people who cared about her? But there was one thing Jennifer had learned about Nicole: It was impossible to predict what she would do.

Then a smile broke across Nicole's face. "Well, if you really want me to—"

"Hooray!" Lisa cried, giving her a big hug.

Eliot smiled. "Good."

"We're glad," Tim said, wrapping his arm around Nicole's shoulders.

"Welcome back," Cathy said. "Now, we'd better hurry up and get back so we can finish up the Comps! The campers are going to go crazy if they get postponed one more time."

"Nicole, come by our office tomorrow, and we'll talk," Tim said. "Okay?"

She nodded. Eliot picked up her one suitcase and started to walk toward his car. "So, how was your hour away from camp?" he joked. "Did you enjoy your vacation?"

Nicole grinned. "It was great. I still don't believe you guys really want me back, though. Are you sure you're not just setting me up for something?" She looked suspiciously at Annie and Jennifer as Eliot tossed her suitcase in the trunk.

Jennifer raised one eyebrow. "Try not to be such a cynic. We happen to want you back, okay? But don't push it."

Nicole shook her head. "I guess I should have bargained a little harder before I said yes. I could have gotten you to agree to do my chores for the rest of the summer."

"Fat chance," Jennifer retorted, and Annie started to laugh.

"I guess everything's going to be back to normal pretty soon," she said.

Lisa and Annie climbed into the backseat. "Are you guys getting in or what?" Eliot asked, starting the motor. Jennifer and Nicole were standing there waiting to see who would get the front seat.

"I get sick when I sit in the back," Nicole said, shrugging.

"It's only a five-minute drive," Jennifer replied, not moving an inch.

"I have an idea. Why don't you both *walk* back?" Eliot said.

Nicole laughed and slid into the backseat beside Annie. "Okay, just drive."

Eliot glanced at her in the rearview mirror. "Did you walk all the way out here, or did someone pick you up?" he asked.

Nicole groaned. "You know that guy who delivers hay to the stables? Jared?"

"*He* gave you a ride? But he always drives a tractor," Annie said.

"Exactly," Nicole said. "It was perfect—driving away from camp on a tractor, going about two miles an hour. It would have taken a *year* to get to New York that way, so I asked him to drop me off."

Everyone started laughing. "Hey, that reminds me," Lisa said. "The hayride's still tonight, isn't it?"

Nicole groaned. "Spare me."

"Oh, come on—you're looking forward to it. Admit it." Jennifer turned around and winked at her.

"Right." Nicole sounded as if she was irritated, but she smiled back. "I just hope they drive a little faster than that tractor."

"Why, are you planning on going somewhere?" Eliot asked, turning into the camp gates.

"No," Nicole said with a shrug. "Not really."

"Good," Eliot said. From the look on his face, Jennifer could tell that her hunch had been right. Eliot was interested in Nicole—as more than just another JC. He really cared about her. In fact, if it hadn't been for Eliot's involvement, Nicole might still be by the side of the road waiting for a ride.

# CHAPTER
## FIFTEEN

Jennifer crouched down at the starting line. When Michael came in, she wanted to be ready. For the final Comps event, each team had chosen ten runners to represent them, ranging in age from eight to seventeen. Jennifer was the anchor for the blue team, and Andy was the anchor for the gray team. He was standing across from her, waiting for Josh Phillips to come in.

Jennifer hoped Michael had made up some ground. Their team had been trailing by at least twenty yards when they went out on the short cross-country course. Although she jogged several times a week, Jennifer knew that Andy was in a little better shape than she.

"Good luck," Andy said as they saw Michael and Josh come around the bend, dead even.

This was it. The Comps was going to come down to one race, between Jennifer and Andy. "You, too," Jennifer said.

"Go, Andy!" Marian screeched from the sidelines.

"Go, Jennifer!" the girls in Cabin Nine yelled. "You can beat him!"

The course wound around the path that circled the lake, and campers had lined up all along it to encourage their teams. Jennifer was nervous, but it was a good feeling—it was the way she usually felt before a sports event when she was competing. Her adrenaline was pumping, and she had all the energy she needed.

Michael tapped her arm, and she was off. She could hear Andy start running a few yards behind her.

"Come on, Jen—you can beat him!" Eliot yelled as she passed him.

But a few yards later, Andy passed her.

"Andy, Andy!" boys from his cabin chanted as he ran past.

Jennifer knew this course well. She often jogged this way—down the hill, up the path around the lake. She tried to pace herself, knowing there was a long incline coming, but she didn't want to drop any farther behind Andy. He wasn't tiring at all. She tried to summon all the energy in her body and surged forward, closing up a few of the yards he'd put between them.

They rounded the final bend and came back out into the sunlight with only ten yards separating them. Jennifer pushed as hard as she could.

"Come on, Jennifer!" Jennifer vaguely heard

Nicole yell her name. That was odd. Nicole wasn't even on her team.

"Go, blue, go!" several campers shouted, spurring her on.

Just as she was about to catch Andy—that was it. They'd crossed the finish line. Jennifer felt as if her lungs were going to burst. She slowed to a walk, taking deeper breaths. At least she knew she'd run the best race that she could have.

"The gray team wins!" Brett shouted, and the crowd erupted into cheers.

"Nice going." Andy patted Jennifer on the back. "That's the closest you've ever come to beating me."

Jennifer smiled. "Thanks. Don't think I've given up, either."

"Oh, I don't," Andy said. "Believe me, I know you better than that!" He was breathing hard, too.

"You ran a great race, too," Jennifer said. She didn't like losing, but losing to Andy wasn't so bad.

Marian ran over, her eyes shining. "Andy, that was amazing. You're a hero! You won the whole Comps for the gray team!"

Jennifer rolled her eyes, then smiled as she watched Andy squirm. "No, it was the *team* that won," he corrected her.

Marian shrugged. "Well, you still looked fantastic. Are you on the cross-country team at school?"

"Yeah," Andy said. "Look, Marian, thanks for coming over to congratulate me, but I really need to talk to Jennifer."

Marian looked hurt. "Well, okay. I'll see you at the cookout tonight, right?" She flashed one of her cutest smiles.

"Maybe," was all Andy would say before he walked away, pulling Jennifer behind him. "Do you have any ideas about how I can get rid of her?"

"No," Jennifer said. "I've been having the same problem myself, actually."

"Really? A camper has a crush on you, too?"

"Not exactly," Jennifer said. "It's Josh Phillips." She hadn't had a chance to tell him yet. Since she'd stopped working at the waterfront, she'd hardly seen him.

Andy burst out laughing.

"Gee, thanks for the sympathy," Jennifer said.

"No, it's just—you and Josh? I can't quite see it," said Andy.

"Neither can *I*," said Jennifer. "That's the problem. And no matter how much I ignore him, he just won't take the hint."

"Want me to talk to him for you?" Andy asked.

"What would you say?" Jennifer replied.

"I'd say . . . 'Listen, Josh, it's not going to work out between you and Jennifer.'" He mimicked a low, theatrical voice. "'You see, I have something to tell you. Jennifer and I are in love.'"

Jennifer hit him on the arm. "Cut it out! Be serious. What am I supposed to do to get rid of him?"

"Could we fix him up with Marian?" Andy wondered. "No, I guess that wouldn't work."

"All I can say is, if he tries to sit next to me on the hayride tonight, you'd better come over and rescue me," Jennifer said.

"Okay, it's a deal," Andy said. "Just as long as *you* make sure Marian doesn't stow away under a bale of hay."

"Deal," Jennifer agreed. Then she ran off to commiserate with the other members of the blue team.

"I'm really glad you're here. I couldn't stand the thought of your leaving," Lisa said. She and Nicole were in their bedroom getting ready for the cookout, which would be followed by the hayride.

Nicole ran a brush through her hair. "To tell you the truth, I'm kind of glad to be back, too." She turned to get a better look at herself in the mirror. "Do you think these jeans look okay?"

Lisa smiled. "They look fine, as usual. Any particular reason you're asking me tonight? For instance . . . Eliot Packard?" she asked.

"What are you talking about?" Nicole replied, pretending to busy herself with her make-up case so she didn't have to meet Lisa's eyes. What did Lisa know about her and Eliot, anyway?

"Come on, you can tell me," Lisa urged. She took a sweater out of the drawer underneath her bed. "I remember how I felt before Michael and I got together. It didn't seem that it would ever happen."

"Eliot and I aren't going to 'get together,' " Nicole said sharply. "He's just a friend. For all I know, he has a girlfriend back in the city." She leaned closer to the mirror to check her mascara. Eliot hadn't mentioned any girlfriend, but Nicole had never asked. What if she got her hopes up for nothing?

Lisa grinned. "But then again, he might not have one. Nicole, is that eye make-up making you blind? Can't you see the way Eliot looks at you?"

Nicole turned around, genuinely puzzled. "Looks at me? What do you mean?"

"You're such a nut." Lisa shook her head. "Here you spend weeks trying to get Gil to flirt with you when it's obvious to everyone that he's only interested in Annie. Then, when the rest of the world knows Eliot likes you, you act as if you haven't got a clue."

Nicole looked at Lisa. "I don't know what you're talking about."

Lisa threw up her hands. "See? Clueless," she complained. "Take Michael's word for it if you don't believe me. He told me this morning that Eliot has been talking about you nonstop for the past week."

"He has?" Nicole couldn't believe it. She turned back uncertainly to the mirror. The same, familiar face looked back at her. Creamy white skin, purplish-blue eyes with long, black lashes, and black, silky hair. Everything about Nicole was the same . . . but everything was different, too.

"You feel the same way about him, don't you?" asked Lisa.

"I don't know," Nicole said slowly.

"How can you not know?" Lisa looked completely exasperated, and Nicole smiled.

"Okay, okay, I give up. I *do* like Eliot. It's just that I've never had a real boyfriend before—I've gone on millions of dates, but so far I haven't found anyone I really like," Nicole admitted.

"Are you serious?" Lisa asked. "*You* never had a boyfriend, either?"

Nicole blushed. "Whatever you do, *don't* tell anyone else. I don't want everyone at camp to know."

Lisa nodded. "I understand. I won't tell anybody."

"Are you sure?" Nicole asked her. She didn't intend to be the laughingstock of Camp Kissamee, now that she was staying.

"Yes," Lisa said. "You know what? I think Eliot's a good choice for you."

Nicole hoped that everything Lisa said was true. She knew Eliot liked her—she could see it in his eyes. She also knew that they had argued so much when they first met because they'd been attracted to each other, though she hadn't been willing to admit it until a few days ago.

Tonight, she wanted to find out how he really felt about her. She was tired of guessing.

"I'm starving," Nicole said as she waited in line for food with the rest of the JCs at the end-of-Comps cookout. "I think I could eat three hamburgers."

Jennifer dropped a spoonful of macaroni salad on

her plate. "Are you feeling all right? Megan, touch her forehead. The sun must have gotten to her today," she teased.

Megan put her hand on Nicole's forehead. "Very sick," she said. "I think she must have that virus that was going around."

"If it gets any worse, she may even eat a hot dog," Annie added with a laugh.

"Can't a girl even want a hamburger around here without everyone getting all bent out of shape about it?" Nicole asked airily, taking some potato chips. "I'm just hungry, that's all. Of course, if I do eat this food, I might end up feeling extremely ill."

They all filled their plates with food, then went to sit under the large oak tree where they always sat for flagpole.

"Just think, you'd be eating at some fancy restaurant in Paris tonight if you'd gone with your mom," Beth said.

Jennifer winced. She'd never had a chance to tell Beth and Megan the truth, and apparently no one else had, either.

"No, they'd still be on the plane," said Megan. "Eating plane food—yuck." She bit into her hamburger.

Nicole fiddled with the strap on her black sandals. "Actually, there's something I need to tell you guys. Everyone else knows already." She paused for a minute. "My mother wasn't really coming to get me.

I asked her to rescue me from here a bunch of times, but . . . she always said no. So did my dad."

"Oh," Beth said. "I'm sorry. I didn't mean to bring up something painful."

"It's okay," Nicole said. "I called her tonight and told her everything. How I was going to run away, then how I almost got kicked out and you all convinced them to let me stay."

Jennifer was incredulous. It took guts to make that kind of confession. "What did she say?"

"Not much, at first. I think she was stunned." Nicole shrugged. "I don't usually get into trouble like that. Then she realized that maybe I'd been serious about being unhappy. She's going to come back a little early so we can have some time together before school starts."

"Wow, that's great," Annie said. "Maybe this whole thing will bring you closer."

"Maybe," Nicole agreed. "But I'm not going to expect much."

"What about your dad?" Lisa asked. "What did he say?"

"I can't reach him because he's traveling today," Nicole said. She laughed. "Actually, that was the best news of all. Mother said she would talk to him for me—explain what happened. That way he'll cool down before I talk to him."

"I don't see why they should be mad at you," Megan said. "You made a mistake."

"Yeah, I know, but they don't see things that way," Nicole said. She took a sip of lemonade.

"My parents are pretty demanding, too," Jennifer said. "I don't think I'll tell them I lost that race today. They expect so much of me when it comes to sports. If I don't come in first, it's like a total waste of a day to them."

"But they support you all the time," Annie said.

"I know, but that doesn't mean they're easy on me," Jennifer said. "I think I know how you feel."

"At least your parents came for Dead Day!" Nicole said.

"Well, they are only four hours away," Jennifer said. She hadn't thought about it until now, but Nicole had seemed a little depressed that day. *Why didn't I ask her to come to lunch with us?* she asked herself. Then she laughed. *That's right—we hated each other back then.*

"What's so funny?" Annie asked.

"Nothing," Jennifer said. "Hey, Nicole, if you're going to eat three burgers, you'd better hurry up. I think Wally's about to run out."

Nicole was about to take another bite, then she stopped. "Don't tell me—you want me to make a race out of this, to see how many I can eat in the next fifteen minutes?"

"No, of course not," Jennifer said with a grin. "I'll give you ten minutes."

Nicole pretended to take a huge bite, and everyone burst out laughing. For the first time all summer,

Jennifer felt as if the JCs were a real cabin. It was a good feeling.

That night, before the hayride at nine o'clock, Nicole went over to Girls' Thirteen for a visit.

When she walked into the cabin, she heard Janet say, "Hey, Mimi. Want to read that book I was telling you about? I'm done with it." Janet passed a paperback to Mimi, who accepted it shyly.

"Looks as though they're being nicer to her," Nicole whispered to Katy, who was sitting on Dee's bunk.

Katy nodded. "They are. At first I thought they were just compensating. You know, their guilt could explain this behavior. But they seem to be treating her like an equal—I think it'll last."

Nicole nodded. For once, Katy's ultraserious manner didn't bother her. Katy was all right, she thought, heading over to Mimi's bunk to say good night. A little on the weird side, but basically all right. "Where's Dee?" she asked.

"She had to run over to the Lodge to make a phone call, so I'm supervising," Katy said. "So far, so good." She grinned at Nicole.

Nicole walked over and sat down on the edge of Mimi's bed. "Hey, how are you doing?"

"I'm so glad you're staying at camp," Mimi said softly. "Does that mean you'll still teach me how to swim?"

Nicole didn't know what to say. Could she ever allow herself that kind of responsibility again?

"After that dumb accident, I know I really need to learn," Mimi added.

"We'll see." Nicole patted her on the arm. "If it's okay with Tim and Cathy, then sure. I will. Jennifer can help you, too, though."

Mimi smiled, snuggling down in her bed. Nicole leaned closer. "Is everything better with you-know-who?" she whispered.

Mimi nodded. "Yeah. They didn't even give me a hard time when my parents called twice today to see how I was doing. And guess what? My parents are coming next weekend! They're going to take the whole cabin out for pizza—you, too."

"That's nice. Thanks." Nicole let her hand rest on Mimi's arm, thinking. So much had happened in the past week, she could barely remember it all. All she knew was that she was happy to be right where she was.

"Isn't it great that our team won?" Mimi asked, her eyes shining with excitement. "I never thought we would."

"Yeah, it's pretty exciting," Nicole said. *For a dumb camp competition,* she added in her head, remembering what she'd first called the Comps. Everyone had told her it was fun, and it *had* been.

Well, everything except the part when she was the human wheelbarrow.

# CHAPTER
## SIXTEEN

"Jennifer, you look great tonight."

Jennifer bit her lip and turned to Josh, who was sitting next to her on the Lodge steps. It was ten minutes before nine, the time when they were supposed to meet for the hayride. Jennifer had been hoping that someone else would show up before Josh, but she was out of luck. It wasn't as if she were wearing anything special—she had on old jeans and a heavy sweater. She hadn't made an effort to look good, partly because she was hoping Josh would lose interest in her if she looked grubby.

"Thanks," she said. She stood up and started to pace around the steps. "I wonder where everyone else is."

Josh cleared his throat. "I was wondering if . . . uh . . ."

"I think I see Megan and Beth," Jennifer said, craning her neck. *Please let it be them,* she thought.

"Before anyone else comes, I want to talk to you," Josh blurted out. "About us."

" 'Us'?" Jennifer repeated. "You mean the group of us? All the JCs?"

"No," Josh said. "I mean, you and me. And how I feel about you. I haven't gotten the chance to tell you really."

Jennifer waved her hand casually in the air. "That's okay. I think I know."

"Really?" Josh's voice squeaked.

"Yeah." Jennifer sighed. "Listen, Josh, I know you like me. As more than a friend, I mean. And you've been really sweet to me lately, especially when I was in the infirmary. I appreciate all the extra attention you've been paying me."

Josh smiled. "That's great! I was afraid you didn't feel the same way about me as I feel about you. But now that you say that . . ." He stood up and took a step toward her.

"Actually, Josh, I . . ." Jennifer paused. This was one of the hardest things she'd ever had to do. Josh was so sweet, and he was looking at her with such a hopeful look on his face. "I was getting to that," Jennifer said. "I do like you. You're nice, and you're cute, and you have a thousand things going for you. It's just . . . you're not for *me*."

Jennifer looked nervously at Josh, whose expression had undergone a drastic change. His eyes were sad, like a lost puppy's, and he was staring at the ground.

"Josh, I really think you're terrific," Jennifer said. "But you and I, well, it's not going to work out."

"Why not?" Josh mumbled.

"We're not right for each other," Jennifer said. "I don't know why, but you have to trust me on this."

"Don't you even want to give it a try?" Josh asked, finally glancing up at her.

Jennifer shook her head. "I'm sorry, Josh. I don't want you to think there's something between us when there really isn't. Okay?"

Josh shrugged. "If that's what you think."

"I still want to be friends, though, okay?" Jennifer asked. She couldn't stand the thought of not being friends with all the JCs, especially when Josh was such a nice guy. She'd liked him a lot, until he started to pursue her. Then he acted too mushy for her taste.

Before Josh could answer, a group of JCs came wandering across the lawn. "Hey, Jen, Josh. What's up?" Gil asked as he and Annie walked over to them.

"Hi, Gil," Jennifer said. Josh was silent. Jennifer hoped he wasn't taking what she'd said too hard. She didn't want to ruin his summer!

"I think everyone's here," Megan said as Michael pulled up in front of the lodge driving one of the camp vans. "Wait a sec—where's Nicole?"

"And where's Eliot?" asked Gil. Then he wiggled his eyebrows. "Maybe they're together, if you know what I mean."

Annie laughed. "Or maybe they didn't hear that we were supposed to meet here instead of at the Barn."

"They'll show up," Jennifer said. "Nicole's always late, remember?"

"Fashionably late, that is," Beth corrected her, and everyone started laughing.

Jennifer glanced over at Josh. He was laughing, too. *Good. I didn't break his heart, after all,* she thought. Annie had been right—the direct approach did work best. Still, it was funny to be on the other end of a crush for once.

Jennifer smiled to herself as she pictured a tiny scoreboard in her head. When it came to finding a boyfriend at camp, she was 0 for 3 so far. It was time to find another game—one she was a little better at!

Nicole was on her way down to the Barn to meet everyone for the hayride when she heard footsteps behind her. "Nicole, is that you?"

She turned around and saw Eliot. He was wearing a black cotton sweater over a white T-shirt and baggy faded jeans with a black belt. He looked handsome, as usual. "Oh, hi," she said, trying to sound as if seeing him were no big deal. They hadn't spoken except to say hi since he'd come to get her that morning.

"So how does it feel, being on the winning team?" Eliot asked, catching up to her.

"Winning team? Oh, right." Nicole laughed self-consciously. *I sound as silly as Marian,* she thought. "Well, I didn't have too much to do with it."

199

"I did," Eliot said. "I lost practically every event I was in." He laughed.

"I guess we're the first ones here," Nicole said when they reached the gates. "Or else we're incredibly late. Maybe we were supposed to meet somewhere else."

"No, we're early," Eliot said. "I went by your cabin, but they told me you'd already left."

*That sounds promising,* Nicole thought. She wanted to thank Eliot for everything he'd done, but she couldn't find the words. Every time she was around him lately, she felt tongue-tied. When she wanted to say something serious, it came out sounding silly. When she tried to joke, she sounded stupid. "Eliot?" she said. "I just wanted to say that I appreciate everything you did. I know you were the one who got everyone to fight for me. I don't know *why,* after the lousy way I treated you sometimes—"

"You don't know why?" Eliot stared at her, confused. "How many times do I have to tell you? Nicole, I like you. A lot."

He took a few steps toward her, and she glanced nervously up at him. "I like you, too," she said.

"I couldn't let you leave, not when I was falling in love with you," Eliot said.

Nicole thought she was going to fall over. "In love with me?" she echoed.

"Yeah, and I've been dying to find out if you feel the same way about me," Eliot said.

Nicole nodded. "I think so. That's partly why I decided not to leave—well, before I got fired."

"Don't worry about that. Just hurry up and kiss me before everyone gets down here and teases us to death," Eliot said.

"New Yorkers are so impatient," Nicole joked, her hands on her hips.

Eliot shook his head and smiled. Then he reached out and touched her cheek. Everything happened so fast. Did she step forward, or did he? She couldn't tell. One minute they were standing there, like statues, staring at each other. The next minute, they were in each other's arms.

Eliot's lips brushed hers softly, and Nicole kissed him back with an urgency that matched his own. Then he wrapped his arms around her waist and pulled her closer to him.

That was when the camp van pulled up, with its headlights shining brightly on the two of them as they were locked in their embrace. Nicole jumped back from Eliot, who started laughing. She could hear cheers and whoops from the other JCs coming out the windows of the van.

"Welcome to Camp Kiss-Me!" Michael yelled from the driver's seat.

"Glad you stuck around?" Eliot asked, grinning.

"I guess," Nicole said, pretending to frown. Then she reached out and took his hand. "No, definitely."

"Come on, we're waiting!" Megan yelled out the front window.

Nicole walked toward the van with Eliot. Never in her life would she have imagined that she'd feel happy about going on a dumb hayride. But knowing that she'd be snuggled in Eliot's arms, surrounded by friends, she couldn't think of any place she'd rather be.